BY DUSK

THE WITCHES OF PORTLAND, BOOK 7

T. THORN COYLE

BY DUSK

Moss breathed, smelling the sweet, clean musk of the cedar, and the rich honey notes of melting beeswax.

Images darted through his mind like schools of fish. Shaggy's face, lit by sunshine. The strobe lights of the dance club. The river. Images of himself, arms in long tubes, locked down to his comrades. Police in riot gear. Shaggy again, eyebrows creased with worry. Cormorants skimming over the water.

He inhaled again, more slowly and deeply, trying not to clutch at the thoughts.

Trying to flow like the river itself.

This is a standalone book in a linked series.
Please note that one character uses they/them pronouns. This is not a typo or editorial mistake.

1

MOSS

The old-fashioned vaudeville house mostly hosted concerts beneath its arched walls and curved, baroque ceiling. But this Sunday night, Temple, the quarterly pop-up club, was packed to the balconies with every Burner, raver, neo-hippie, and polyamorous love-bomber within driving, cycling, or bus range.

Lights flashed, strobing from blue to orange to white. The DJ, like some sort of God up on the stage, orchestrated it all. The space filled with the sweet tang of marijuana smoke, patchouli, amber resin, gin, and spilled beer. This mélange was undercut with traces from people vaping near the door, and Moss loved it all.

It was everything that Moss's spirit desired. He needed this more than anything else right now. A moment of joy. A chance to feel free.

The electronic dance music pulsed through Moss's body, lighting him up inside. There was nothing, absolutely nothing, that he loved better than this. To be surrounded by a crush of other humans, all moving, flowing, sinuous, and staccato. One being, made of light and sweat and joy.

With a roar, the crowd raised their arms, and shook their hands in the air. The beat shifted, the bass kicked in, and like one dynamic creature, the whole crowd began to bounce. Sheer joy. Moss's smile was so huge, it felt as if his face would split in two. Lifting his own arms, he slid his fingers through the air, feeling the spirits. The hundred-year-old spirit that lived in the building. The spirit of the sound system and the lights. The spirit of the music itself. And the spirit of each person as they danced around him.

Moss bounced, and waved his hands, conjuring up a spirit of his own. A spirit of magic and love. His calves bunched and tightened, shaking him up off the long, wooden planks of the dance floor, bouncing with the rhythm of every single body that touched his. Yes, this was his religion. Yes, as much as he adored the magic of his coven, and the sacred beauty of the great outdoors—the rivers and mountains and trees—this was Moss's church. It was here that he prayed.

A nerdy, activist, Japanese-American kid from Beaverton, he'd become an EDM fan the first time his parents took him to the Portland Pride parade. He'd never gotten around to asking whether his parents were just trying to share their culturally liberal stance with their only son, or whether they'd somehow picked up that his crushes included a girl in his class and Tobey Maguire in his tight Spiderman suit.

That June day, the sight of men kissing men, women kissing women, and folks of indeterminate genders frolicking around in outfits that would make any cosplayer proud had made his head swirl. But the biggest soul-shaking thing about his first Portland Pride? That was the music.

It boomed from party floats festooned with ribbons, balloons, and streamers and covered with happy people gyrating in the sun. The music filled him with a sense of happiness he'd never experienced before. In the decade since, it didn't matter what the dance music called itself—EDM, house, even industrial—or what variations came and went on the charts, Moss sought it out.

So here he was at Temple. The place of worship. The place of delight. The place where Moss, packed in with a thousand other people, could worship as he willed.

Moss needed church. It had been a hell of a year, and frankly, the last giant piece of magic his coven had done had depleted everyone. Oh, it was well worth it—they'd pretty much taken out the whole infrastructure of Immigration and Customs—but the coven needed a break. Except for one meeting to debrief, Arrow and Crescent Coven hadn't even met. Not even for the full moon. And here it was, coming up on the autumn equinox, and Moss couldn't help but wonder what was next.

Lately, something tickled at the edges of his awareness, breaking through the pulsating sense of well-being and joy. It was the same thing that had been bothering him off and on for the past couple of months. Trouble brewing. A spirit in danger. Something...

Whatever the spirit was, it didn't feel like one of the smaller, more ordinary kami that inhabited everything. This consciousness felt big. Moss had been so exhausted and overwhelmed he hadn't made space to figure it out yet, but it felt as if the kami was part of some large system important to Portland itself.

As he danced, his thoughts traced the edges of the troubled spirit. Sometimes it took an altered state like being on the dance floor for his subconsciousness to rise to the surface, giving him the information he was seeking. He danced, pushing just a little at whatever it was...and a sudden rush shot through him, as if a dam had burst, shoving him off balance.

Moss stumbled into the man next to him, a white dude in dreadlocks wrapped with Day-Glo yarn. The man gave his arms a friendly, steadying squeeze.

"You good, gorgeous?" The man flashed him a huge grin, white teeth glowing green beneath the black lights.

"Um. Yeah!" Moss shouted back, shaking his head to clear it. "I'm great. Thanks."

He *had* been great, anyway, until that energetic river practically knocked him to the floor.

"Is it you?" he murmured, conjuring up the image of the Columbia River that bordered Portland in the north, dividing it from Washington state. "Or you? Are you trying to tell me something?" The Willamette River. The body of water that flowed closest to Moss's home. He considered that river a friend.

Neither river gave him much, just an increased sense of unease. But he couldn't help but feel there was more going on. That his spidey senses hadn't been telegraphing danger for nothing.

But damn it, he needed a night off from all of that, which was why he'd come out in the first place. *Be here now,* as the hippies would say. Moss shook his head again, then shook the rest of his body in time with the beat, trying to get back to the moment, and dancing, and not worrying about the past, or what might be coming.

If he were a different person, he would be dissolving acid on his tongue, or dropping MDMA to escape what worried him. But the magic of the music and the energy of the crowd were ecstasy enough. He had learned that long ago. Oh, Moss wasn't against some of Snoop Dogg's "Tanqueray and chronic," and would be getting another drink or a puff soon, but for joyous, soul-expanding communion? His preferred drugs were still sex, magic...and dancing.

When trouble dogged the edges of his consciousness, any of the above were usually an antidote to his woes. Tonight, he let the music move all thought out from his head, and opened his own spirit outward again, reveling in the flow of the music and the crowd.

The DJ segued into Moss's current musical favorite, Kygo. The bouncy tropical house mix filled the air with quick piano, electronic backbeat, and over it all, soaring, R&B tinged vocals. Moss threw back his head and laughed.

On he danced, twirling and bouncing, bumping shoulders, and tasting the sweat that rolled past his lips. If he could have kissed the entire universe, he would.

It was good to be alive.

Forty minutes later, Moss was soaked in sweat, feeling cleansed, and vibrating with the power of the crowd. He also desperately needed some water and a little breathing room. He angled his shoulders, dancing his small frame through the crush, toward the long bar lit up with blue and white lights.

And then he saw her. The dream girl, with her pale, elfin face, lightly muscled shoulders, and sharp collarbones that peeked out from a bright silk halter top. His two-night stand from the massive Bliss Festival up in British Columbia just six weeks before.

He'd volunteered to work the big camping festival to get out of town, away from the political aftermath that rocked the city after the coven and their friends had taken down the ICE building and freed the asylum seekers into the loving, capable hands of a whole network of immigrant's rights groups.

Oh, it had been a righteous action, but Moss needed

some frivolity after that. His work as both an activist and a witch got too heavy sometimes.

And at Bliss, he'd found her. In between his work shifts, they'd danced for hours, bumping against each other over and over, until finally, they ended up making out while several thousand people danced around them. Moss would never forget that night. The massive energy of the crowd. The way the music felt like sex. The way her lips tasted, like pot and cherry candy.

Finally, she had dragged him back to her fancy glamping tent, lit with glow sticks and solar lanterns. Back to her bed, piled high with fake fur blankets and tapestry pillows.

Who had a tent like that? A bed like that? Moss was lucky to have his one-person—two in a pinch—crawl-in-on-your-belly tent that he took on bicycle trips and back-packing.

But yeah, at a festival where Moss had to work in exchange for the price of a ticket he couldn't afford, who had a fancy tent like that?

A rich girl, that's who.

A tiny woman with strawberry-blond hair in a pixie cut, and lips he wished he could kiss again.

A woman named Shaggy, that was who.

All thoughts of the river, agitated kami, and any trouble that brewed in the early autumn air left his head when she turned, and the strobing lights of the club lit up her blue, blue eyes.

2

———

SHAGGY

Shaggy felt out of sorts, despite being in the middle of a dance party where some of her favorite music played. Well. It had been her favorite music until recently. Damn it. Now, the bouncy birthday ode to Kygo's baby girl just made Shaggy want to run.

And she wasn't actually in the middle of the party, either, more like skirting the edges tonight, and that wasn't like her. She shouldn't have come out, but had thought the scene would take her mind off her current problem. But now that she was here—not drinking, not smoking weed, or dropping Molly—all she wanted was to go home to her newly purchased condo in the Pearl, dodgy stomach, tender breasts, and all. Her mother had bought the condo as an investment, of course, but it was Shaggy's while she got her MFA.

"Buy you a drink?" The man was tall, with dark skin barely covered by a green vest that topped his loose, paisley-patterned pants.

"Oh! No. I'm just waiting for my friends. Thanks, though."

One of the little lies that every woman learned to tell strangers. Always let them know you have backup coming, even if you don't.

"You have a chill night," the man replied, before turning away.

Finally, the hated "Happy Birthday" song ended, the DJ put on some old Skrillex, and the crowd went nuts. From just outside, it looked like some giant, undulating sea creature made of Day-Glo and neon in the midst of a great, dark sea lit from above by cosmic forces gathered in a riot of celebration.

And not too long ago, Shaggy would have felt all of that, too. She would be high, and smack in the middle of the cosmic party.

But she was new to town, having just moved up from California wine country to go to design school in a place far enough from her mother, but still close enough to remain within her sphere.

She had no posse, no squad, no gang of brightness to surround her and jolly her out of her current mood.

She was pregnant and didn't know what she was going to do about it, and it was all her fault. She was the one who'd stupidly forgotten to pack condoms and insisted he didn't need to go back to his tent for his stash. He said he was clean, and she replied that she was both clean and on birth control even though the latter wasn't true. She barely ever *had* periods and had more scar tissue in her uterus than any one person should be subjected to. Doctors repeatedly told her it was highly unlikely she'd ever get pregnant. But then she'd started feeling nauseated, and suspicious. Three positive home pregnancy kits later, and here she was. Sore, alone, and pregnant by a person she'd had sex with three times over the course of one music festival. A person she would never see again.

Might as well get drunk, she thought. No way was she keeping this thing inside of her for nine months anyway, so why was she even being careful?

She knew why, though. After being told your chances of pregnancy were slim to none? You didn't easily throw away what might be your only chance.

But that didn't make her want a baby. Not now, and after resigning herself to her situation, she had assumed, not ever.

"Hey! Shaggy! Wow! What are you doing here?"

Oh shit. What the *hell* were the odds? It was him, with his practically black eyes, his short shock of black hair, and his soft, warm voice. Standing there, staring at her with a look of happy surprise on his face, a bottle of water in one hand. The activist and great dancer. The guy who looked amazing, all pale brown skin and tight muscle in a white tank top that glowed lavender under the strobing lights.

The guy who kissed like no one she'd ever kissed before.

Moss. The guy who'd gotten her pregnant.

"Shaggy?" His gentle hand on her upper arm. "You okay?"

"No, I..." Heart racing, she whipped her head around, looking for a way out. It was all of a sudden really hard to breathe. "I need to get out of here."

"Let's go," he replied, and gently steered her through the people clustered near the bar and around the edges of the main dance floor. Pushing through the double swinging doors felt like entering an airlock. Instantly, the sound muted itself and the pressure on her heart and lungs receded.

But Moss didn't stop. He continued through the small,

jewel-like vestibule and on out through the heavy glass and brass doors.

Shaggy followed like some imprinted duckling. Shocking as it was to run into him, she had to admit it was nice to see his face. But fuck, how the hell was she supposed to have a normal conversation with the guy when a tiny elephant occupied the space between them?

"Need some water?" he asked, cracking open the cap.

She nodded and, taking the plastic bottle, raised it to her forehead for a moment before drinking. Cool. Wet. Good. It calmed her jitters a little. She handed the bottle back.

"Thanks."

Two couples tripped down the sidewalk toward them, shrieking with laughter. A car boomed by. The air smelled of motor oil and the lingering scent of perfume. Moss angled himself toward her, just a little. Not enough to seem like he was protecting her, but just enough to let her know that yeah, he was there.

He smelled like clean sweat, cinnamon, and sunshine.

"So, um..." she said. *Great, Shaggy.* But she really didn't know what else to say, and then realized he was talking.

"I never expected to see you again," he was saying. "What are you doing in Portland? I thought you lived near SF?"

"I do. I did. I came up to go to design school." *And to get away from my mother, Bianca, who only wants the best for me and thinks I'm halfway useless.*

"Wow. That's cool."

"What are you doing?"

"Me? Oh, just gig economy stuff, you know. Picking people up in my hybrid, making deliveries, and spending the rest of my time trying to save the earth."

He grinned on that last part.

"And going clubbing." Shaggy jerked her head toward the doors.

"Always," he replied. His eyebrows drew together slightly. "But we got you out of the club because something was going on. No pressure, but do you want to go somewhere? Talk about it? I can buy you a drink. Cup of tea, maybe?"

She stood rooted to the sidewalk for a moment, staring at him. Part of her wanted to run back to her posh condo. The other part wanted nothing more than to have a cup of tea with this guy.

Even if that meant she was going to need to figure out how to get through the next hour while lying through her teeth.

Because no way was she telling Moss she was pregnant.

For one night, this night, she was going to pretend to be a woman who'd run into a really nice guy she'd had some fun with at a festival. That she wasn't pregnant and running from weird family shit. That she wasn't rich and he wasn't poor. She'd act as if maybe, just maybe, they were a couple of regular people getting to know each other over cups of tea in a café at night.

3

MOSS

M oss parked on a side street near one of the swank restaurants across from the river on the edges of downtown.

He'd been driving all morning and needed a break. Taking a deep drink of water, he wished his steel thermos was filled with coffee instead. Oh, he knew the water was more important, and his body needed it, and yadda yadda, but the reality was that he'd gotten only three hours of sleep. The cup of coffee he'd made at home felt long gone, having barely penetrated his system.

He and Shaggy had talked for a couple of hours, closing out a late night café. It was great to see her. To smell her. She clearly felt troubled by something—skirting around a big topic, it felt like—and getting her to laugh a couple of times had felt like victory. Once they'd been kicked out by a sleepy barista, Moss walked her to her place, a condo complex further north in the Pearl. She didn't invite him up, but the place looked as high end as her glamping tent.

After an awkward hug goodbye, Moss walked back to his car and drove across the bridge toward home, completely amped up and had stayed that way until he finally nodded off in the middle of an old Bruce Lee movie at around three-thirty in the morning.

He still couldn't believe he'd actually run into Shaggy after resigning himself to never seeing her again. A woman who...yeah. A woman who did him in. Who might just be someone special.

He glanced at his phone, which was plugged into the dash. The battery had been draining itself lately, and he didn't know why. The thing just wasn't that old. He also hadn't made the time to take it in. The phone was practically brand new, no way it should be draining that way. He'd been getting weird spam texts and a higher than usual level of robot calls, too. Should he check with Alejandro or Jack to see if someone was messing with it? Or was that too paranoid?

Moss sighed and unplugged the phone. The battery was at fifty percent and would have to do.

Shoving open the door to his second-hand Prius, he groaned. He really felt like hell.

Count your blessings, man.

The ginkgo trees that lined the street were beautiful, the sky was blue, and he'd had a great time the night before. An amazing night, actually. Better than expected. And he wasn't stuck in an office cubicle, which made life even better.

And right this minute? One of his blessings was the fact that he could take a break, get some more coffee, and take a walk along the Willamette. The Prius beeped as he locked it. Moss had bought the used car with a little help from his parents. He felt bourgeois and weird driving the thing, but his dad pointed out that if he was going to drive for a living, he might as well pollute as little as possible. As an environmentalist, Moss couldn't disagree.

Someday, he'd like to do something that felt more right-eous for work, but for now? Driving paid the rent on a big bedroom in his shared St. John's household, and left him time to do tree sits, blockades, and other actions.

Shoving his key fob into the pocket of his jeans, Moss strolled up the sidewalk toward the coffee cart at the corner. Just up ahead, beneath one of the trees, a houseless man stuffed a big, black coat into a collapsible shopping trolley. It was his old friend, Henry. The man had the long, tapered fingers people usually associated with pianists or basketball players. Moss happened to know he'd been the former, and still played when he could in community centers or the occasional bar that actually let him through the doors.

That was how Moss had met him. Henry was playing for tips in a dive bar in Moss's neighborhood one night. He'd still had a room indoors then, at a single room occupancy hotel, so it was easier for him to get the occasional gig. His playing was sublime, and Moss had thrown some money in his jar and then ended up talking with him for an hour once his sets were done.

"Hey, Henry!"

"Moss! It's good to see you, my friend!"

"How you doing?" Moss asked. Henry looked okay today. Just a little worn out around the edges, like his coat, but rela-tively clean, and clear-eyed, too.

"I'm alive, my friend. It's another beautiful Portland morning!"

"I was heading for a coffee. Can I get you something?" Moss nodded toward the cart one block up, toward the river.

"A black coffee and a banana wouldn't go amiss."

"You got it," Moss said. "Come on down once you're packed up."

Moss really liked the man, but running into him also

hadn't been part of the morning's plan. He really wanted some alone time at the river, and now it seemed like he might not get it.

The universe doesn't always give us what we want or need, but sometimes it does, and we just aren't paying attention. Raquel's words echoed inside Moss's head. His mentor was pretty wise sometimes, and she was right. This was probably one of those moments Moss needed to pay attention to.

He paused under a ginkgo tree for the space of one long inhalation. *Hello, tree*, he thought, then softly clapped his hands three times. The greeting and hand claps were ingrained habit—it was just polite to greet the kami of a tree you were standing under—and he didn't wait for a response before closing his eyes and sending his next thought further out into the cosmos. *May I be open to what this moment has to teach me.*

A diffuse sort of prayer, it was more of a reminder to himself than an entreaty to anything else that might happen to be listening.

He heard Henry's cart trundle up behind him and snapped his eyes open again, smiling and feeling a little more centered and less grumpy than he had when he'd parked his car. Worked like a charm.

"You doing your witchy business?" Henry asked when he reached Moss.

"Something like that. Let's go get that coffee."

Moss placed their order at the little red kiosk, paid, and then turned to Henry.

"Hey Henry, how has the city felt to you lately?"

He wouldn't ask just anyone a question like that, but Moss knew Henry kept his ear to the ground and would understand what he meant. Even in his worst drinking bouts, Henry generally kept his wits about him. He was also one of the most perceptive people Moss had ever met, outside of his coven mates.

Henry ran a hand across his stubbled chin, thinking.

"Moss!" the cart owner called. Moss returned to the window and retrieved two cardboard coffee cups and two bright yellow bananas.

He joined Henry on a piece of low wall that edged a restaurant parking lot and faced across Naito Parkway toward the river. It wasn't as good as being directly next to the river, but the view was gorgeous nonetheless.

The span of the Burnside Bridge gleamed to his left, its low white observation turrets looking down on the river. On the water itself, past the greensward of Tom McCall park, sailboats tacked under the morning sun. The air was warm, but not hot, and the coffee had a delicious, nutty taste to it.

Henry carefully unpeeled his banana and took a big bite. This gave Moss a pang. The guy was clearly hungry, and had probably been packing up to head over to Sisters of the Road for lunch.

"I'm not keeping you from something, am I?"

Henry shook his head and chewed. "Nope. I need to head out soon, but I've got a little time. You wanted to know if I noticed something strange lately? About the city?"

"Yeah. You know, like people being more agitated than usual, or more fights breaking out...or the opposite, even. More people in a good mood. Like that. Or the crows or geese acting differently, even. I know you spend a lot of time on the streets and around the river here, so I figured you would notice."

Henry finished his banana and carefully set the peel on the wall before picking up his coffee cup and taking an appreciative sip.

"Abdul makes the best coffee," he said. "To answer you,

yes. I think I have noticed some things lately. It feels like there's more pain in the air than usual, if I can put it that way."

Moss sipped at his own coffee, thinking. As he drank the nutty brew, he centered himself again. Dropping his attention deep into his center of gravity on a breath, he focused. Then, on his second exhalation, he imagined the edges of his aura softening, and let his attention expand all around him. It was hard to do, because he felt so tired, but it was a technique that Brenda and Raquel had drilled him in. Clearly he needed to practice more but...Henry was right. There was something there.

"It makes sense to me, Henry. I feel it, too."

The city felt...disturbed. And what was worse? So did the river. Damn it. He really needed to get another hour's worth of driving in before his lunch date with Alejandro.

Whatever was bothering the spirits of the city and the Willamette would have to wait. And Shaggy? He just hoped she'd see him again.

4

———

SHAGGY

Shaggy found it very hard to focus, which was bad, because the class wasn't all that large and there was no place to hide. She was one of only twenty people in the bright room, and despite the lights being off and the roller blinds all at half mast so they could watch the examples Professor Logan clicked through on the white screen, the mid-September sun still streamed through the windows.

It was early fall in Portland, Oregon, and here she was, in school again. She loved school. She'd been totally looking forward to getting her MFA in creative design, with an emphasis on costumery, even if it meant she had told her mother she would also take some UX classes. As if she wanted to work for some corporate user experience department. But she did it to keep the peace. And to get a break from the family dynamic without cutting herself off so much that the money dried up.

Professor Logan was an older white guy in a faded denim shirt and black jeans. With bright green rectangular glasses perched on his nose, he looked like some Boomer hipster. His hair was a short white shock that contrasted with his salt-and-pepper goatee. The snatches of lecture penetrating Shaggy's swirl of thought and emotion were actually interesting. His hands swept through the air as he explained the history of designing furniture that combined both form and function, whether it was making patterns for large, industrial produced mass-market chairs or hand-building a single sofa.

But she couldn't pay attention. Couldn't get the pregnancy thing off her mind. That damn Kygo song from the club still bounced through her head, reminding her that she should be overjoyed to be pregnant, instead of angry, annoyed, and confused.

Gah. This was the last thing Shaggy needed. She'd gone to the club hoping to escape her news for a few hours, not have "you're pregnant" thrown in her face. And then Moss. She'd forgotten he lived in Portland, if she'd ever even known. Seeing him felt like a punch in the chest. Her body still wanted him. Badly. And the longer they talked over their late night tea, the more Shaggy had to admit that her heart wanted him, too.

But she still had no clue how to navigate the situation. She'd moved up here hoping to have a chance to actually live the life of the free spirit she pretended to be. The raver rich girl with the weird name, whose mom, Bianca, paid for fancy electronics and VIP passes to all the big festivals. Bianca hated Shaggy's world, including her "little hobby" of making clothes, but she paid for it all the same.

No one ever saw the cost, or the grief that had almost ripped Shaggy to shreds a year ago. No one knew that Shaggy had basically cared for her once-famous father all during high school after Bianca had abandoned him to alcohol and depression.

Bianca paid both for his condo and his basic monthly

bills, of course. "I'm not heartless," she would say. But she wouldn't see him. The divorce was finalized by the time Shaggy turned sixteen.

So Shaggy had become his only confidant as his hands —which once wielded the sculptor's tools that gave him worldwide recognition, now ruined by rheumatoid arthritis —only held a constant glass of gin.

A few days before the massive heart attack that killed him, Shaggy stopped by his condo. "My heart is broken, little girl," he'd said to her. And one week later, they'd found out that was true. He'd left Shaggy to Bianca, who indulged Shaggy's grief by letting her club her brain out as long as she went to university and got some sort of degree.

Well, Shaggy had done that, studying art history and fiber arts, then trying her hand at figure drawing, before settling on huge, abstract paintings done while high on ecstasy or smoke and making festival costumes for herself and her friends.

But she needed to get away, from Bianca and from all the places she'd known only with her dad. So she had applied to the Portland School of Design, figuring it was both just far enough away to escape, and close enough for Bianca to not complain.

And now she was pregnant.

And Moss...

Professor Logan switched his slide to something so perfect, Shaggy gave a small gasp. It was just a chair, and clearly an assembly line chair, at that. But Shaggy could still feel the artist in it. She could see their vision in the graceful curve of the back, and the way it fitted just so into the rounded seat. And the legs...arcs of wood so slender, she wasn't even sure how they supported anything, let alone a human body.

But there it was. Possibility. Creation.

She realized her hands had crept over her still-flat stomach muscles. Damn it.

Damn it. Damn it. Damn it.

What the hell was she going to do with...all of this? It hardly seemed fair. She was twenty-two years old, finally free of emotional responsibility, or so she had thought.

And then, class was over. The blinds snapped all the way up, flooding the room with sun. Shaggy blinked. Professor Logan shut down his computer, and Laura, the nice Brazilian woman close to Shaggy's age, was headed up the aisle toward her, a big smile on her deep brown face. She wore orange overalls over a white T-shirt, and looked absolutely gorgeous. Laura swung a backpack over one shoulder, and paused by Shaggy's table.

"Shaggy! You look as if you've seen a ghost! Are you going to yoga today?"

"Oh! Um...maybe. I hadn't thought about it." She fumbled her tablet case closed, and shoved her things into an oversized teal leather shoulder bag.

Shaggy paused, then looked up at Laura's expectant face.

"Actually, do you have time for lunch or something? Or dinner after yoga class?"

Laura looked pleased. "Yes. I would like that. Dinner after yoga, I mean. I have another class after this. Meet at the yoga shala, then?"

Shaggy wondered if she'd kept herself way too distant from people for too long. She'd just gotten used to hiding while taking care of her dad. Who would ever believe the poor little rich girl who had all the money and drugs a person could ever want had troubles of her own?

Maybe it was time to let her guard down. Her intuition, a thing she paid attention to only when it grew frantic enough to scream—like when it told her she had to move the fuck away from Marin County—was telling her yes, to let Laura in.

Or at least to try.

"Yeah. That'd be great! I...really need to talk to someone and I don't have friends here yet."

Shaggy didn't really have friends anywhere, she realized. And she hadn't for a long time.

"I'm always happy to listen," Laura replied, giving Shaggy's arm a slight squeeze.

"See you at the studio then," Shaggy replied. The other woman smiled, and began to walk away. Shaggy looked around, at the empty tables and chairs. Professor Logan and the other students had already left the room.

She was alone again. But maybe, just maybe, she didn't have to be.

5

MOSS

Moss opened the door onto the lunch rush at Raquel's café. The place buzzed with conversation, the milk steamer going, cups clattering, and over the speakers, Janet Jackson was joining the rhythm nation. Dang. He should've gotten here sooner to snag a table, but had gotten pinged for one last drive that he couldn't resist. Under capitalism, money was money, and a guy had to eat. He crossed the black-and-white-tiled floor and got in line. Most of the tables in the center of the room and all of the booths against the wall were full, plus the café was clearly doing takeout for folks on a break from work. They lined up and down the center aisle, waiting for coffee, pastries, and grilled panini.

The place smelled of coffee and toasted cheese sandwiches.

"Hey Moss!" Raquel said with a harried smile as she rang up the person in front of him. The line had moved forward while Moss wasn't paying attention. A gorgeous Black woman a decade older than him, Raquel wore her dreadlocks tied back in a red scarf. "Your latte will be right up, Cherise."

The woman moved to the side, making way for Moss at the counter.

"Hi Moss!" said Cassiel. A white woman around Moss's age, with a ponytail that kept a riot of red hair off her face as she expertly foamed milk and poured espresso shots. She and Raquel both wore red aprons over T-shirts and jeans. The aprons picked up the red in Raquel's signature coffee cups.

"What's up, witches?" he asked. Raquel was co-founder of Arrow and Crescent Coven, and both he and Cassiel were members. "I'm meeting Alejandro. He asked me to order. So, two panini specials and I want a large coffee and whatever Alejandro gets. He said you'd know his poison."

"That would be a double cappuccino, oat milk," Raquel said, ringing him up. She leveled her dark, all-seeing eyes at Moss. "You make sure he pays for this. Man makes five times what you do."

"At least." Moss fished for his wallet and slid his card into the chip reader. "How's Zion, he doing okay?"

"Happy to be back in school, though not as happy as I am!" Raquel replied. "And yeah. He's doing okay. The kids who were bullying him transferred out, and he's got more backup now."

"That must be a relief. It's good to have a little victory now and then."

"You're right about that. I gotta get back to it."

Moss nodded and turned to look for a table. Three people were exiting one of the booths. He slid onto a padded bench beneath a cool watercolor of two red-winged blackbirds. The art in Raquel's was always shifting, done by local artists trying to sell their work to folks who would never see it otherwise. Moss appreciated that about Raquel.

She always supported community in as many ways as she could.

The whole coven did, really. Moss wouldn't hang with them, otherwise.

He'd been raised by Buddhists. His dad was white and his mom was Japanese American and they'd met on a Soto Zen retreat five years before Moss was born. His mom's parents had taught him some Shinto, and told him stories about the Ainu, the aboriginal peoples of Japan. As a teenager, he did more study on his own, and started making offerings to the kami, trying to pay attention to the spirits of everything around him.

His parents encouraged his spiritual practice, though their eyebrows sure had raised when he joined the coven. He still hadn't figured out a good way to explain it to his parents...how all of his meditation, and his offerings to the spirits of place—and to his phone and computer even—helped his life. And that all of it had led him to wanting to study magic. If Arrow and Crescent hadn't been down with social justice, and were only a bunch of middle-class white people, no way would he have become a witch. But along with their commitment to justice, they were also one of the most mixed groups a person could find in seventy-five-percent white Portland, Oregon.

And over the past couple years? They'd become his friends.

Alejandro strode through the door, neatly pressed in black trousers and a crisp orange dress shirt. He was an in-demand IT guy with such mad skills he could've dressed however the hell he wanted. He actually liked dressing like a businessman. Said it gave him a power edge when he had to deal with uber-wealthy white assholes.

His face was lightly stubbled, needing a shave, but his

formerly shaved head had thick hair growing back on top, dark and gorgeous, shot through with a few silver strands. Round tortoiseshell glasses framed his eyes. He was handsome as all get out, and knew it. Moss grinned. He loved that Alejandro was relatively rich, pansexual like him, Latinx, and a witch to boot.

It gave Moss hope for the world, and for himself, personally.

He held out his fist, and Alejandro bumped it with his own.

"Cassie's waving. I'll go get our drinks." Alejandro slid his brown leather folio onto the booth table before heading to the counter.

He was back in a flash and set a giant red mug in front of Moss before sliding onto the bench across the table with his cappuccino. Then he grabbed a twenty from his wallet and held it out.

"Lunch is on me."

"Dude. You don't have to pay for the whole thing. Just give me a ten."

"Dude. I'm a rich Marxist. From each according to their ability and all that. Just take it. Please."

Moss took the money. He didn't make nearly enough driving strangers in his car to argue.

Raquel set the panini sandwiches down. "Here you go!" she said and hurried back to the counter. They really needed three people during rush, but there was no room behind the counter, and Moss knew Raquel couldn't afford the extra help, either.

Alejandro sipped his cappuccino and sighed with appreciation.

"What'd you want to talk about?" Moss asked.

Alejandro nodded, then swiped a hand over his hair, slight frown marring his handsome face.

"The river. One of my prospective clients is..." His voice trailed off and he picked up his grilled panini. Cheese oozed out from between the toasted bread.

"One of your clients is what? And which river, exactly?" Moss's sense of uneasiness returned. He knew exactly which river Alejandro meant, but had to ask, just in case he was wrong. Portland had two main rivers: the Columbia, which skirted the north of the city, and the Willamette, where he'd been that morning, which divided the city unequally into west and east.

"The Willamette." Alejandro leaned across the booth, sandwich still in hand. "And I can't talk about my prospective client. I'm already under an NDA...."

Moss picked up his own panini and chewed. He felt impatient, but Alejandro would get to whatever he could talk about in his own time. Moss was no stranger to classified information, though his secrets were all about security culture to keep activists safe from the FBI and right-wing doxxing, not corporate espionage.

Oh yeah...grilled peppers, mushrooms, and Jack cheese, all sandwiched between crispy grilled bread. So good. He shouldn't be eating cheese, but lactose intolerance be damned, sometimes he just had to have it.

Alejandro finally spoke. "But I thought your people should know...you might want to test the water again."

"Are you *kidding* me? We just got the worst of it under abatement last year! You telling me there's something new? Or just new levels of some of what we've already been pressuring the EPA to clear up? You know they don't want to pay any more, right?" This was worse than Moss had feared.

Alejandro gestured for Moss to lower his voice.

Moss flung his sandwich onto the plate and picked up his coffee. He gulped two huge swallows down.

"I hope you're not taking this fucking client."

Alejandro looked irritated but shook his head. "Of course I'm not. Do you think I'd be telling you anything if I was?"

Moss deflated. "Sorry, man. It's just frustrating, you know. I mean, we've worked so hard to get the polluters out and hold them accountable for cleanup. And you know it affects my neighborhood the worst."

Moss's neighborhood of St. John's hung on to its status as an African American neighborhood by its fingernails. The neighborhood was established during Portland's old redlining days but was rapidly paling as white folks figured out there were historic houses to be had for half the price of other parts of the city. Albina, one neighborhood over, was already mostly white, despite the BBQ joints and Black barbershops that still peppered the streets around Mississippi, MLK, and Rosa Parks Way. Everyone else had moved further east, across 205, and into the numbers. Portland needed more affordable housing, and fast, but NIMBYs and YIMBYs were in a deadlock with the city and each other.

Alejandro nodded. "Look, I won't be able to provide counsel this time, because of the damned NDA, but I can get you hooked up with people if you need them."

Moss wiped his hands on a rough brown napkin. Part of him wanted to punch something, and part of him wanted to cry.

"It's just so frustrating, man." He looked at his coven brother. Behind his glasses, Alejandro's eyes just looked sad. "When are we going to catch a damn break? It's one thing after another these days. I mean, all the shit that's gone down here in the last year alone. Plus the yearly West Coast fires... Haven't humans done enough damage? Really? Do we really have to poison *everything*?"

Alejandro slid a hand across the table and gripped Moss's right hand, forcing it out of the fist he hadn't even known he was making, and wrapping their fingers together.

"We're a mixed bag, good and bad. The Divine Twins, circling each other. It's our job to make sure things at least stay even, right? Keep tipping the balance back."

"It just breaks my heart, you know. Plus...I'm tired."

And all of a sudden, he was. Dancing and seeing Shaggy were only a temporary reprieve from his heartsore exhaustion. Moss needed a break. A *real* break. The whole coven did.

But it didn't seem like that break was coming anytime soon.

6

SHAGGY

Shaggy and Laura sat in one of the padded window booths at a Peruvian restaurant in the Pearl. They both had a glass of sparkling water and one of a crisp Sauvignon Blanc to hand, and ate roasted corn kernels while waiting for their dinner to arrive. Shaggy liked the design of the place. The booths managed to be both comfortable and contemporary, with slanted backs made of three different colors of leather, nestled next to floor-to-ceiling industrial windows. The ceiling had open wood beams that glowed under perfectly placed spots and dangling pendants made of curved balsa wood.

If she ended up not doing costume design, she'd love to design a place like this someday. But *having* a baby right now meant moving back to Marin, taking time out from school, and basically, rethinking her entire life.

And not having a baby right now? It meant she probably would never have a child at all, unless she adopted. Shaggy sighed and took another sip of wine. Hints of apricot and pine nuts. It was so crisp, she could practically bite it.

Yeah. The thought that she shouldn't be drinking—and

why—drove her toward the wine. Not a great coping mechanism, but here she was, anyway.

The ashtanga yoga class had been intense, which was good. Being forced to place her full attention on flowing through the sequence at a pace quick enough to make her sweat had kept Shaggy's mind quiet. Her body was loose now, and despite the glass of wine to hand, she felt a little stronger, more centered, even. That was a good thing, because if she had to make a big decision, she needed to feel as together as possible, and not like the complete wreck she'd been since her gynecologist appointment.

"How long have you been in Portland?" Shaggy asked.

"Fifteen years. My father moved here to work for Nike, so I practically grew up here."

"Do you ever miss Brazil?"

Laura shrugged. "Sometimes. We go back at least once a year, though, to visit family. Nike keeps threatening to send my dad back, now that they're expanding over there. But both of my parents have grown used to Oregon. Part of why I'm in design school is so I'll have more options if the family moves. These big companies can use people like me to take care of what they call 'emerging markets'."

"How do you feel about that, though? I mean, is that a good thing? Being at the mercy of what your family wants?" Bianca was in international finance and Shaggy wanted nothing to do with it. Whenever that came up, her mother was quick to remark that Shaggy didn't mind having her bills paid, did she?

Shaggy figured she more than deserved to get her bills paid for putting up with Bianca and for taking care of Dad for all those years.

"It's no better or worse than anything else in this world, you know?" Laura said. She paused as the waiter set down a series of small dishes in between them. Shaggy's stomach growled as the smells hit her. There was spicy fresh fish, potato and chicken causas, and beef empanadas. The hearts of palm salad looked good, too, but it was all Shaggy could do to not shove a whole empanada in her mouth with her hands.

She forced herself to be polite and act as if she wasn't ravenous. She'd thrown up her breakfast and hadn't been able to eat since. Pregnancy. She felt like shit, the scent of coffee was the worst thing in the world, and then she wanted to eat everything in sight.

After Shaggy and Laura both dished some of the food onto their plates, Shaggy gestured to Laura to continue.

"Brazil has been so poor, for so long. And everyone exploits her. So big corporations bringing actual business to the country, instead of just extracting resources? That feels okay to me. And if I can help some locals make some reals"—Laura pronounced the word *hay-ows*—"all the better, you know?"

They ate in silence for a moment.

"But what about you?" Laura asked. "You said there was something you needed to talk about?"

Shaggy stopped chewing, the soft potato and chicken causa turning to sand in her mouth. Damn it. Why did she have to feel so afraid?

Because Bianca made sure you knew that discussing your personal business with strangers was forbidden. And that you should really just keep your feelings to yourself. Her mother hadn't always been that way, but after it became clear that her dad couldn't make art anymore, and had sunk into his depression, she just...went away. And expected Shaggy to go away, too.

So Shaggy just pretended to be a party girl and hid her

terrible secret away: her father was drinking himself to death and her mother was slowly turning into a bright and brittle monster.

Shaggy cleared her throat and took a sip of wine. It tasted sour. She drank some more.

"I'm pregnant," she blurted.

Laura raised one well-manicured eyebrow, and tilted her head toward Shaggy's glass.

"I take it you don't plan to keep it?"

"That's just it," Shaggy said in a rush. "I don't know. I mean..." God, how much was she going to unload on this poor woman?

Laura took a bite of fish, and chewed as if she had all the time in the world for Shaggy to figure out what she did or did not want to say.

"I mean, I don't want a baby. Not now. And I'm not sure if ever. But thing thing is? I thought I couldn't even get pregnant. I've had all of these..." She took another sip of wine. "...complications. Doctors all said it was super unlikely. But here I am, pregnant anyway."

"Does he know?"

Shaggy shook her head.

"I barely even know the guy. He was a festival hookup, you know? Although it turns out he lives here."

"No! In Portland? And you did not know this?" Laura leaned close, face alight, ready to gossip. "Is he cute?"

How long had it been since Shaggy had a friend to gossip with? Probably not since eighth grade. Too long.

She gave a wry grin. "He's too damn cute, actually. And I really like him."

"That's great!"

"No. You don't understand," Shaggy moaned. "That only makes it worse."

Laura popped a piece of empanada crust into her mouth. "Worse how?"

"If I didn't like him, it would be easier to just not tell him anything. But it turns out, he's actually a pretty cool guy. So now I have to make a decision."

Laura picked up her wine glass again. "Girlfriend, you don't have to tell him any damn thing you don't want to. If he was your boyfriend it would be different. But he's not. It's your body, and your life."

"It's still part his, though…"

Laura *hmphed* at that, waving a hand in the air, as if brushing away a gnat. "How far along are you, even? I can't see anything, even in your yoga pants."

"Six weeks."

"It's barely a blip! The size of a seed!"

Shaggy sat back against the booth and looked out the window. People hurried by, carrying packages from nearby shops, or hefting purses and leather satchels, heading back to their condos after working downtown.

She glanced back at Laura, who drank her pale wine, staring at Shaggy.

"Wait. You're Brazilian. Aren't you supposed to be Catholic or something?"

There was that hand wave again. "We're half Catholic, half Spiritualists, like two thirds of the people in Brazil. But my mother is a nurse. She raised me to be practical about such matters."

Shaggy ran her fingers over the bare wood of the table, feeling the edges. Looking for something solid to hold on to. Her stomach turned sour and she pushed her plate away.

"Shaggy. What do you want?"

Shaggy looked at her new friend. "I don't know. I

thought I did, but now?" She shook her head, her mouth filled with sudden sourness.

"Excuse me..." Stomach lurching, Shaggy shoved her way out of the booth and ran toward the women's room. She hoped she made it in time.

7
___

MOSS

"You make the best garlic bread, Maggie." Tariq practically groaned. The tall, thin activist had been living in Justice House—a huge, rambling, four square Craftsman—for a few months, and so far, was fitting in just fine.

"Thanks, Tariq!" Maggie padded into the living room/dining room combo from the kitchen, carrying a big bowl filled with mixed greens and the tuna salad Moss had put together when he got home. She wore her signature jeans and a white, button-down men's shirt that skirted her frame. A bit butch, their Maggie, in contrast to her girl-friend, femme-as-fuck Barbara Jean. Cis and trans, butch and femme, both white, and both radical as anything.

As a matter of fact, if anyone could be said to be more radical than Moss and Tariq, it was probably Barbara Jean, who was a fierce part of the local Black Bloc anti-fascist contingent. Masked up and out in the streets with Roses and Thorns was the only time you'd catch Barbara Jean in pants and boots.

"Where's Barbara Jean?" Moss asked, after Maggie

settled herself on one of the three mismatched armchairs clustered around the coffee table.

Moss sat on the wood floor, leaning up against a battered couch that had seen better days. Once upon a time it had been a nice, overstuffed sofa with a blue fitted cover. Now it was covered with a striped blue and green bedspread and swamped with throw pillows, courtesy of Maggie and Barbara Jean.

"She should be here soon. Had to work late at the hotline. Why? Did you need her for something?" Maggie took a big bite of her salad. "Hey, this tuna's good tonight, too. Spicy."

Moss grimaced. "I got some news today, and figured I'd wait 'til all of us were here to talk about it."

"Personal?" Tariq asked, setting his garlic bread down on the round white plate on his lap.

"It's about the river," Moss said, and shoved some of his own salad in his mouth before he launched into his worries. Their house was pretty close to the Willamette. He lightly tapped his fork on the edge of his bowl three times, softened his attention, and with a *reach* of his psychic senses, connected with the spirit of the river. He could feel its distress, and it made him unhappy. He shoved more tuna into his mouth and started wishing he had a beer.

Their household had a loose "don't drink and light up all the time" agreement with one another. It wasn't that they didn't like to party, but they also tried to adopt as much militant discipline as they could most of the time.

"We need to be ready to roll at any moment," Barbara Jean would say. And she was one-hundred-percent correct.

Moss still wanted a beer. Instead, he focused on chewing his food, and tried to slow his anxious jitters down. Breathe. Chew. Swallow. Breathe.

Moss set down his salad fork, picked up his own garlic bread, and took a big bite. His eyes practically rolled back in his head. "Oh my Gods and Goddesses, Maggie. This is even better than usual!"

Maggie beamed, her pale, freckled face lightly flushed up to her dyed red hair. "I added fresh oregano and rosemary into the olive oil before throwing it into the oven."

The rattle of keys at the big wood Craftsman door announced Barbara Jean's arrival.

"Honey, I'm home!" she called out from the entry way. Moss heard a rustle and pause, then the clump of Barbara Jean's backpack on the ground, followed by the double thump of her ubiquitous chunky heels. Justice House was strictly a no-shoes household, by Moss's request. The housemates had soon decided it was worthwhile to have to clean less, and had installed shoe and boot shelves in the foyer.

Finally rounding the corner into the living room, Barbara Jean's cheerful, made-up face brightened at the sight of her housemates. She wore a colorful flowered dress beneath a black jacket and, even with her purple-and-black streaked hair in disarray, looked like a thousand thrift store bucks.

"There's garlic bread and salad!" Maggie said.

"Hooray!" Barbara Jean replied, pausing to give Maggie a kiss on the forehead before scuffing off to the kitchen in bright red slippers, flowered dress swirling around her calves.

"Would you bring me a beer?" Moss asked. Barbara Jean leaned her head back into the living room, one eyebrow cocked.

Moss just shrugged and shook his head. "I'll explain in a moment."

"You *sure* it's not personal?" Tariq asked again.

"Not personal, but it sucks, and makes me feel tired."

The not personal part was half a lie. Seeing Shaggy again had really affected him, but he'd have to deal with that some other time, if at all. Despite having exchanged numbers, there was no guarantee Shaggy would even want to see him again.

Barbara Jean shuffled back in, carrying a filled plate in one hand, and a six pack of beer in the other. She sent both down on the long coffee table and plopped herself down next to Maggie.

"I figured if the news was upsetting enough that you needed a beer, we may as well all have one."

Moss grabbed a beer, snicked the top off with the church key on his key ring and took a long pull on the local IPA. He had tried to hate IPAs, given their history as a colonial beer, but sometimes a person had to let the past be the past and enjoy the present. Right? It was a good enough excuse for a beer he loved.

Besides, everything in life was tainted with post-colonialism and late stage capitalism....

"Earth to Moss!" Maggie rapped her rings on her own amber bottle, disrupting his thought spiral.

"They're fucking up the river again. It looks bad. I got an inside tip that we should get the waters tested again."

"Well, shit," Barbara Jean replied. "How quickly do we need to act? And what does this mean for the equinox celebration under the bridge?"

Local members of the American Indian Movement and the Clean Rivers Coalition worked with other local indigenous leaders on a twice-a-year water blessing in the shadow of St. John's Bridge. Moss had attended a time or two, and it was pretty cool.

"Damn," he said. "I forgot that was this weekend."

Which was stupid. As a witch, he knew it was the equinox, so of course the water blessing would be happening.

"I hate this, man! Those greedy fuckers need to stop spilling their messes in our 'hood!" Tariq's fork clattered back into his bowl. "I'm ready to lock down, man, for as long as it takes."

"I'm with you, man, but Barbara Jean is right, we need to check with the First Nations before we start planning any actions. We don't want to step on their event." Moss took another sip of beer and closed his eyes. The Willamette still whispered on the edges of his skin. He set down his beer, clapped his hands three times, and found the still point that rested below his navel.

Then he reached, seeking information.

The river was present, but wasn't interested in talking today, at least not in words. He deepened his attention. *The important thing was...* Moss's eyes snapped open, and he looked at the faces of his housemates, comrades, and friends.

"No matter what, we need to remember to work with the flow and not against it. We need to not face these people with fire, but with water."

"Whatever you say, man. I don't understand your witchy shit, but fire or water, we have to do something."

"We just need to figure out what that is," Maggie said.

Moss held up his beer bottle. The other three followed suit.

"To the Willamette."

They clinked their amber bottles together and drank.

8

SHAGGY

Shaggy had every window in her one-bedroom Pearl District condo wide open to catch the evening breeze. The air had been warm all day, with the feel of late summer about it, but was rapidly cooling, and felt good on her skin. Portland, it seemed, wasn't one of those places where a hot day equaled a hot night.

Shaggy danced. The music was bright, with a deep bass holding up the beat. Her face wet with a mixture of tears and sweat, she bounced around the rust velvet upholstered sofa, and the two teal damask armchairs arranged in front of the white-tiled gas fireplace that she had fallen in love with when she and Bianca had first toured the place. She had imagined herself cozied up to the fire in wintertime, drinking tea or wine, or sharing a joint with some newfound friends.

Now she didn't know if any of that would ever happen. Shaggy wanted to run, and when she felt like that, the easiest thing to do was dance until her fight or flight impulses calmed down and she could think again. Puking had put a damper on dinner with Laura. Despite the woman's sympathy, Shaggy hoped she actually understood, and wasn't just making polite noise. Shaggy really needed a friend right now.

"Why the hell did I move to Portland?" She shouted the words over the blasting EDM, still bouncing and swaying, flicking her fingers to the beat and waving her arms in the air.

If she hadn't picked Portland, the choice to have an abortion would have been easy. Well, not easy, given her personal physical complications, but easier. If she hadn't picked Portland, she wouldn't be dealing with Moss. He never would have to know. But now?

It didn't seem right to not tell him, but...she really didn't want to have that conversation. Not at all.

And given those physical complications? She still didn't want to deal with the fact that this pregnancy might be her only chance to have a child. Trouble was, she'd already given up on the thought of children. She'd done the work in therapy around it. Made her peace. She'd even begun to look forward to a life of freedom from responsibility for other people—not her father, not Bianca, and not a brood of kids.

She could design clothing. Run away with the circus in a tiny house. All the things she was already doing in some small way.

Shaggy had just been waiting for...something. She wasn't even sure what. For Bianca to chill enough to not threaten to cut off Shaggy's trust fund anymore? For her to gain enough skills in the design and circusing departments to make a real go of it?

Or to find herself while still semi-cocooned?

Shaggy gave a noisy exhale at that last thought, lips making a motorboat noise in disgust. She bounced herself to a console against the white entry wall and thumbed the music up. Maybe it would drown out her damn thoughts.

Dancing over to the black-metal and glass windows, she looked out over her neighborhood. People rushed by, heads down, en route home from work. Others streamed into the restaurants and bars that dotted the revitalized neighborhood. "Gentrified," someone like Moss would call it. She was sure he lived in some politically correct, hippie trash heap with ten other people, like any righteous person would.

He'd given her such shit about her glamping tent.

"All this is for you?" he remarked when she pulled him inside the softly lit canvas bell tent. If she hadn't already been halfway gone with desire, she might have kicked him out, but her body knew what it wanted, and it wanted it right then.

So Shaggy had let the comment slide, figuring she'd never see the guy after the festival anyway. The sex was so good, they did it again. And again.

And now she had some of his cells inside her. Damn it.

What would it be like to be with him? Like, to really be with him? Getting to know each other. Sharing space, even. Talking for hours. Kissing for more hours. Trading off making breakfast.

Shaggy realized she'd stopped dancing. She shook out her hands and feet, and stretched, then tried to find the beat again. Her feet faltered. It wasn't happening. Maybe she should go out to the bar one block away, the one with handsome-looking men and women clustered on the sidewalk, enjoying life. Like she should be. She could drink whiskey and flirt. Or maybe even get into an interesting conversation, like the kind she went to grad school for.

Instead, she walked across the room, turned the music

off, then walked into her blinding white with steel-and-black-accents kitchen and clicked the kettle on for tea.

"This isn't fair," she said to all the brightly colored boxes in her tea drawer before fishing out a bag of spearmint and grabbing a blue mug from one of the cupboards. The mug was painted with white swirls, and she'd gotten it at yet another festival in Marin.

Nothing in life is fair, Bianca would say. But what would her mother know? She hadn't been the one who had stayed and taken care of Shaggy's dad when he was at his worst. She knew Bianca was impatient with Shaggy's "free spirit life" as she called it, but again, what did she know?

Nothing.

Bianca had no clue how badly taking care of Dad had messed Shaggy up. So what if she needed to lose herself while living in a paid-for condo for a few years? It wasn't as if Bianca didn't have the cash to bankroll everything.

The kettle clicked off, and Shaggy plopped the tea bag in the mug and poured steaming water over the top, breathing in the minty steam.

But maybe Shaggy didn't want that anymore, either. Maybe she wanted to take care of herself, she realized.

"And how's that going to go down?" The room had no answer. She shook her head in disgust. Maybe she didn't know shit, either. Maybe no one did.

Shaggy took her tea to one of the windows and leaned out, staring downtown to her right, and over at the buildings toward the river and the Morrison Bridge straight ahead. Then, leaning out, she looked down at the grid of streets, and the people. For one wild moment, she considered dropping the heavy mug out the window. She could hear the satisfying smash it would make on the concrete sidewalk.

The tea would splash in all directions, leaving a dark stain behind.

She pulled herself back inside and shut the window, then dumped her tea out in the porcelain sink and sank down to the kitchen floor.

"What the fuck am I going to do?"

9
____

MOSS

Moss paced himself next to Terra, smelling the brackish scent of water and skirting seagull and cormorant droppings. They walked on the east side of the Willamette, because Terra's job was over that way. It was a gorgeous, late September Tuesday afternoon and the air was still warm, and Moss was in his standard uniform of black cargo pants and slogan T-shirt. Today's simply read "Fuck War." Terra was dressed in jeans and an orange blouse that complimented her dark brown skin. Her face was bare as usual, and she'd recently cut her tight curls into a cap that framed her skull.

Despite the beauty around him, Moss felt restless. Anxious. It was hard to match Terra's measured pace.

Terra had just gotten off from the non-profit she did web-based marketing for. She also ran their social media accounts. It was only part-time, and she filled in the rest with the small salary she got doing the work of her heart— direct action trainings with the Hue and Cry Collective. They trained people all over the United States, and even traveled the world. Terra mostly trained people in the Pacific

Northwest in things like consensus process, banner drops, and blockades.

Terra was a radical Black woman and pretty bad ass. She and Moss had met during a wave of anti police-brutality actions and had even toyed with dating. After a couple of post-action rounds of feverish sex, they finally decided they were better paired as action buddies. They'd been organizing together ever since. Funny, he ended up that way with a lot of activist friends. They toyed with attraction and sex, and then decided it was going to get in the way of the work that needed doing.

And Moss always ended up alone. Maybe the fact that Shaggy was so outside the sphere of his day-to-day world was a good thing. Maybe... *Focus, Moss.*

He exhaled, and simultaneously tried to tune in to the kami of the Willamette, calm his jitters, and explain to Terra what was going on.

"There's a new polluter in town. And my source says they're being backed up by two of the other corporations we hamstrung a year back. They're shunting ammonia and PAHs into the water and its only a matter of time before the bass, salmon, and catfish start dying again."

"And the herons, gulls, and cormorants. And the seals. Plus, the kids getting rashes again." Terra got into a fighting stance and threw three quick punches at the air. "Damn these greedy pigs, anyway."

Moss didn't reply. The more he thought about what Alejandro had told him, coupled with the disturbed waters of the Willamette, the greater his sense that there was something besides the corporation at work here. Some other being that had its own agenda, maybe connected to the corporation? An egregore, maybe? He'd need to check in with the coven about that.

Egregores were a type of magical being, an amalgamation of thoughts, energy, and emotion. Sometimes they were made on purpose, with intention, and sometimes they formed themselves by accident, through all the ways that humans made things: with half-thought words and strong emotions, through fear, or lust, or love. Whether made with neglect or some perversion of desire, the creatures limped through every family, every marriage, every political party, every football club, and every corporation.

Some egregores had a positive impact on the world, or on relationships. Others? Not so much. And the capitalist machine was full of them.

They were branded by names and logos. And they had a purpose, even if the people who had formed them did not. These magical beings—these egregores—acted as ambassadors and representatives. They cajoled and enticed. They made a person feel as if they belonged, or as if owning a new watch or car or the latest game was their right. Or as if maybe, just maybe, that promised thing would complete them.

Moss and Terra resumed their walk, skirting the fire house where the rescue boats launched, and walked out on the little esplanade that looked directly over the water. Leaning on the square metal railing, they watched a barge move slowly by.

It felt good to stand quietly for a moment, to get in touch with his breathing, and find his center once again. Between Shaggy and the polluters, Moss needed all of the centering practices he could get. He slipped a strand of prayer beads from his wrist and began a round of meditative prayers. *Hail wind, hail sun, hail river, hail land,* he thought as the wooden beads slid between his thumb and pointer finger. *Hail spirits of place. Hail those who have gone before. Hail those who are yet to come.*

As he ran through the simple litany, Moss sent a deep exhalation through the soles of his feet. *Hail, Willamette.* Beads still in hand, he softly clapped three times, and sent his consciousness in search of the kami of the river. He felt the disturbance of the barge's motor. Felt the cars rumbling across the many bridges that spanned the water.

He felt the poison slowly slipping through the molecules of water. *How can I help you?* he asked. The kami stirred, as if it was attempting to reach him. Or to figure out who this creature was that kept calling it, and why it was speaking.

"So, when do you want to do the action?" Terra asked, breaking through his reverie.

Moss blinked at the sun-dappled water.

"Equinox." He slipped his prayer beads back onto his wrist.

"Equinox? Isn't that this Saturday?"

Moss gave his friend a wry smile. He knew he was a shit, but he also knew that timing was key.

Terra narrowed her eyes. "You never want to give a sister time to prep folks, do you?"

Moss blinked at the sun-dappled water again and shook his head. "What's the fun in that? But yeah, it needs to be equinox, because of the event on Saturday that we should coordinate with. You know, the Clean Rivers Coalition, American Indian Movement, and some other groups always do that equinox river blessing."

"Have you talked to the elders yet?" Terra's dark eyes looked troubled.

He didn't blame her. Saturday's event was supposed to be a celebration of all the coalitions getting the river closer to being actually cleaned up. That was another thing that made Moss feel like a shit: he was going to have to break it to them that the waters weren't so clean after all.

The kami of the river whispered, but he couldn't quite make out the voice. *What are you saying?* he thought. A seagull screamed overhead, and out in the dark waters a fish slapped the surface before disappearing in a ripple of concentric circles.

"I haven't yet; all of this is just coming out now," Moss replied.

"We're going to have to get permission for this. You know that, right?"

He sighed and turned toward her. "It's next on my agenda, Terra. I've got a meeting set up with the Yakama and Chinook elders and some others. If you have time, it would be great to have you along."

"Just let me know when, I'll be there."

Both activists looked back toward the river, leaning on the rail. The river looked beautiful, the bridges that spanned it carrying people and goods, buses and cars, bicycles and walkers. The Columbia and Willamette rivers gave Portland both its name, and its life. So why in the hell were people hell-bent on killing them? Moss knew the answer to that, and he always had.

But that didn't mean he had to like it. And it didn't mean he wouldn't fight the bastards with his dying breath.

10

SHAGGY

Another warm day. It was so warm, in fact, that Shaggy had put on a sundress, trying to jolly herself out of her nerves.

It was one of her favorites, a pale blue with sprigs of white branches in a repeating pattern. She'd sewn it herself in high school. Standing near some concrete benches in the middle of the quad, she gazed up at a small stand of Douglas firs tucked into a corner of the quadrangle. Inhaling the scent of sun on concrete and trees, she decided she could really get used to the wide variety of Pacific Northwest trees. Towering firs, spreading oaks, ginkgo biloba, with maples and dogwood leaves turning gold and red. California neighborhoods tended toward monoculture with their trees if they had them, and every freeway sprouted billboards, while up here, the sides of the roads were a sea of green.

She rolled her shoulders and her neck. Damn, she was tense. She felt nervous, out of sorts, not the laughing, confident person who had dragged Moss into her bed. She looked around at the groups of students wandering by, messenger bags slung over their shoulders, cups of coffee in their hands, and wished, just for a moment, that she could trade places with them, knowing full well people looked at her and thought the same. It was all an illusion. How much could you really know someone else anyway?

She tapped one sandaled foot and checked her phone for the time. Moss still had two minutes before he was late, so why this impulse to run away and pretend he was a no-show?

She rolled her shoulders again. Maybe she just needed more exercise. She'd signed up for private tutoring at a circus school off Hawthorne Street, but really needed to get back to regular group classes. Maybe she could convince Laura to check the place out one day. She missed being on the silks, feet and arms wrapped in the long swaths of fabric, head thrown back, the closest she'd ever been to flying. She missed the sense of freedom that it gave her. Missed the connection to her strength, too. The few tutoring sessions she'd made it to so far weren't quite enough.

Right now she wasn't feeling either strong or free.

Yeah. Maybe she *should* run away. Like, really run away. Indulge her late night tantrum fantasies. She could have the abortion, call it quits at school, and fulfill her circus dreams. Buy a tiny house, hitch it to a truck, and get the hell out of town. Even without Bianca's help, she could make it, at least for a while. She was a good enough seamstress to make festival clothes and if she could pick up work as a performer on the way...

Shaggy ran her fingers through her short pixie cut, then dropped them to her sides. *Who are you kidding, Shaggy? You need a lot more training for anyone to hire you as a performer, and yeah, people like your clothes, but it's not as if you have any business sense.*

But was that her voice, or Bianca's?

Shading her eyes with one hand, she scanned the quad again. And there he was, sunlight shining on his black faux-hawk, walking with a confident lope. A smile creased his face when he caught sight of her.

Damn. She inhaled a breath so huge it felt as if she were breathing in the whole world. How in the hell could a man she should probably be running far away from affect her like that? She needed for him to not affect her that way.

How was she supposed to deal with this entire situation? All of a sudden, she resented her father and Bianca for taking away her chances to make close friends.

She could really use someone who knew her, right about now. Maybe Laura would become that, but...

"Hey Shaggy." His voice was low, and his breath smelled of mint. "It's good to see you."

"Let's walk," she said. They walk past the concrete benches, and toward the series of grassy, tree-filled squares known as the South Park Blocks. Moss seemed a little distracted, but also happy to see her. His hand kept reaching out to brush her arm, which made her squirm.

The words she needed to say to him were shoving at her lips, and her tongue, but she couldn't speak them. Not yet. And the more he touched her, the more confused she got.

She jerked to a stop in the middle of the quad. "Moss. Stop. Please."

He dropped his hand and stepped back, concern and confusion warring on his beautiful face.

"I'm sorry. I should have asked permission to touch you. But after the other night, I thought..."

"It isn't that." Shaggy crossed her arms over her chest, hands gripping her upper arms as though she were clinging to a life raft, or as though she stood in the middle of a blizzard instead of in the middle of campus on a beautiful, sunny autumn day. "I have something I need to tell you, and you're making it really hard."

The sun bounced off Moss's hair. His fauxhawk gleamed like a crow's wing. He stood, arms loose, completely still. Waiting. All of his attention was focused on her. She'd never had that kind of attention before, except, come to think of it, one of the times they'd had sex at Bliss. It was their third round, and they'd both gotten over the initial "rip your clothes off and do as many hot and acrobatic things as possible" rush.

Moss had slowed things way down, and began massaging her, rubbing the scented oil she'd bought from one of the vendors into her skin. He started down at her feet, paying attention to each toe. To the spaces in between her toes. To the balls of her feet. Her arches...on up he went, so slowly. Carefully.

With intention.

That's how he looked at her now. As if it was his intention to hear every word and every space between each word.

Shaggy didn't even know such a thing was possible. Her father had been pretty absorbed in his own misery, and Bianca barely listened to her at all.

Poor little rich girl. The thought flickered through her head before she could stop it. Her constant refrain. Her "people would kill for your life" reminder. Shaggy's way to cut herself off from feeling anything real.

And now, here was this man, standing in front of her, real as could be. And she felt it. She felt him.

"Do you need to sit down?" he asked, voice so quiet she had to strain to catch the words above the noises of skateboard wheels and cars, of conversations and music playing from the student café a few yards away.

Shaggy nodded. She did. She did need to sit down.

"May I?" he asked, holding out one hand. An offering.

She nodded again, and unhooked her fingers from her upper arms. He gently took one of her hands and led her through the quad, as if he knew exactly where he was going.

He was so certain. More certain than she currently felt about anything. Shaggy let herself follow.

It was funny. Her mind had been so hectic ever since yesterday. But right this second, she felt calm. As though a door had just opened inside of her.

The trouble was, she still didn't know what was on the other side.

Moss brought Shaggy to his favorite tea house. He could tell she was upset, and just hoped she would tell him what was up. He got her settled in one of the benches that lined the far wall, against a great tapestry that hung practically ceiling to floor. Moss loved this place. There were plump fabric cushions in muted colors everywhere, and low tables. It was a perfect place for lounging, hanging out, drinking tea, and having the sorts of conversations that wandered and rambled over the course of a few hours.

He had a feeling it wasn't going to be one of those kinds of conversations. Too bad. He would like to have one of those conversations with Shaggy; he would love to tell her about the actions he had planned, and find out what her hopes and dreams for the future were.

Who are you kidding, man? he thought as he got in line at the counter. He looked out one of the giant plate glass windows, barely seeing the sun shine or the people walking by. *You, the guy who's never made a commitment to anyone? The guy who always says saving the earth is more important than any person? You want to know someone's dreams for the future?*

Thing was, he really did.

He ordered a pot of gen mai cha and two tiny porcelain cups, and threw in a few almond cookies too. As he picked up the laden tray and walked towards the table, he realized he was worried about Shaggy. She seemed like an automaton. Except for the fact that she was still hot, he could barely see the woman he'd met at Bliss. Shit. He had too much going on to deal with whatever this was. To deal with her. But he also couldn't walk away. He couldn't treat anyone that way, let alone a woman he'd had sex with.

He settled himself on the bench next to her, but far enough away to give some space. After the distribution of tea cups and napkins, he finally poured tea from a round metal pot into the little porcelain cups. It should have steeped a little longer, but he just needed something to do.

Remember, Moss? Bruce Lee. Be like water. The teaching of a Chinese martial artist? Or the Willamette itself? Didn't matter. It was all the same.

He took a long, slow breath and tried to relax, focusing on the teacup in front of him. Steam swirled up, carrying the scent of green tea and toasted rice. This was his favorite tea, and had been since he was a teenager.

Shaggy sat stiffly on the bench, leaning as far away from him on the silvery green and brown cushions as she could. It was clear she wasn't ready to talk yet. Okay. Small talk. He could do this.

"I never got around to asking you before, why Shaggy?"

"My name? When I was little, I really, really, liked Scooby Doo, and my dad said I was always rushing head-long into trouble. He's the one that started calling me Shaggy, and then it just stuck."

"How about now?"

"How about now, what?"

"Do you still rush headlong into trouble?"

She looked down at her teacup and frowned.

Great. Just great. Now he felt like an ass.

"Okay. Sorry. Change of subject..."

She waved a hand at him, as if to say "it's okay" but he could tell it wasn't. So, he began to babble. About how cool it was to see her. To reconnect. About all the places in Portland she should visit. About Mount Tabor. And hiking on Mount Hood. About a secret creek he knew....

"I'm pregnant." She blurted the words out fast, as if she could slip them into the space of Moss's inhalation. Her right hand flew up to her mouth, trying to catch the sharp sounds that had burst like a raptor going in for a dive, ready to hook a fish.

Moss's body jerked. Hot tea splashed over his hand. He set the cup down, mopping at his hand, his jeans, her sundress. Her beautiful, pale blue dress.

His mind was a jumbled tumbling of thought and no thought, sound and no sound. It was roaring. A roaring that made no sense. A roaring that...

"Moss? I'm kind of freaking out here." Her voice finally penetrated the white noise inside his skull. "Stop."

Stop. That word again. He looked down. Oh. Her small, pale hand was on his. Clutching at it. Jerking on it. Trying to get his attention as he clutched a soggy paper napkin and frantically mopped at her dress. Gods, how long had he been doing that?

He disentangled their hands.

"I'm sorry. I guess I... Pregnant." He sat back against the cushions and threw the half-shredded napkin on the table. "You're pregnant. I thought you said..."

He finally looked at her. Really looked. Her face was flushed, her eyes bright with tears. She grabbed a napkin off the table and wiped her eyes, then blew her nose.

"I know. It's messed up. didn't know whether I should tell you," she said. "I almost…"

He leaned towards her, closer, but not too close. He could hear the pant of her breath, close to panicking. He could smell her. Lilacs. "You almost what?"

"Left." She looked across the crowded café, out the windows, a crease between her brows. "I almost just left."

She sounded forlorn, and a little bit lost. Moss wanted to wrap his arms around her and hold her close, try to make her feel safe. He also wanted to run out the door as fast as he could, and never stop.

He took in a shuddering breath, then picked up the teapot again and poured them both more tea. They needed time, and tea helped everything. Holding her cup out towards her, he forced himself to wait. She finally looked his way again, startling a little at the offered cup.

"Thanks," she said, taking it from his hands and raising it to her pale, unadorned lips.

He drank his own tea, small cup warm beneath his fingers, tasting the nutty rice and the sharp, spring-grassiness of it, trying to calm himself down further. It was all he could do to keep his feet still on the floor. He pushed air into his belly, slowing his breathing down, trying to connect to the kami of the floorboards and the tea. But could he connect to the spirit of the woman sitting next to him?

How could he not? At least a little. She was warm, and he remembered the softness of the skin across her exposed collarbones. Remembered her tiny feet. But would she want him to connect to her?

Would she want to link with him? The thought brought

the image of the two of them on her bed in that ridiculous fancy tent. He felt his face grow warm, and took another quick sip of tea.

He swallowed. Cleared his throat.

"So, do you, umm, have a plan? I mean, I'll support whatever you want. I should've said that right away, I'm sorry I didn't, it just…"

"It just freaked you out?" she asked. The left side of her mouth quirked up in half a grin. It wasn't a real smile, but he would take it.

"Yeah, it freaked me out. But seriously, just tell me what you want and I'll do my best to show up."

Her eyes darted between the teacup in her hands, his face, the plate glass windows, and back to the teacup again.

He leaned closer again, trying to catch her gaze. He decided to take a risk, and reached out to touch her arm. "I mean it, Shaggy. I'll do my best to do right by you."

"And why should you?" she asked. "I told you I was protected. It was just supposed to be sex. We were never even going to see each other again. There's no way you have any responsibility for the situation."

Her voice sounded half panicked, with a tinge of bitterness.

He shifted on the bench, drawing one knee up so he could face her head on. "None of that matters," he said, and realized that it was true. "What matters is right now. Do you want an abortion? I'll go with you. Do you want a kid? We'll work out the details of how that might look."

She had lowered her head, trying to avoid his gaze. But she raised her eyes to him then, and licked her lips.

"I'm not sure I want a baby. But it's complicated."

"So tell me about it," he said, and poured them both more tea.

He was acting much calmer than he felt, but that's what stand-up guys did. Right? Made *holy fuck* situations not all about them.

Shaggy grabbed her purse, face creased. "I...I can't do this, Moss. I'm sorry. I thought I could but..." She shoved her way up from the table.

Moss half stood, hands out. "Shaggy, wait. I just want..."

"I'm sorry, Moss. I'm sorry." Blue sundress swirling around her pale calves, she wove her way through the tables.

Moss sat back down and slammed his hands his thighs.

Damndamndamndamn. Shaggy. The woman who meant something. She'd left. She'd just left him.

And he'd just watched her walk away.

12
—————

SHAGGY

Laura was ensconced on Shaggy's rust velvet sofa, shoes off, feet tucked under herself, glass of Malbec in hand.

Shaggy had a glass of the red wine at her own side, but was at the dining table that looked into the living room, fabric scraps around her, sewing machine whirring as she pressed the foot pedal down.

This evening, she needed conversation, wine, and creativity all at once, and had decided, fuck it, she was going to get all three. Laura had said she was willing to listen, and fortunately she was also willing to hang out in Shaggy's space, drink her wine, and stare out the big windows at the lights of the Steel and Burnside bridges.

Maybe Shaggy would figure out how to make a friend after all.

She wasn't sure if her need to sew costumes and festival clothes was a sign that she leaned toward the "run away with the circus" end of the spectrum, or if she just felt the need to have a tiny bit of control over one part of her life.

She and fabric had an understanding, and working with the trusty little machine always helped somehow. The colors and textures soothed her, and, pattern or no pattern, the halter tops and loose pants were put together in a way that made sense.

"I notice you're drinking wine again tonight," Laura said. "Does that mean you've made a decision?" Her lightly accented voice was high and a little bit tinny, which still startled Shaggy. Looking at Laura, she expected the woman to have a deeper voice, though she had no idea why.

Shaggy's foot froze on the pedal, causing the thread to snarl on the orange jersey fabric under her hands. She swore under her breath, snapped the presser foot up, and turned the wheel on the side of the machine to lower and raise the needle. Gingerly, she extricated the snarled fabric until there was enough slack to snip the threads.

That done, she looked at her new friend, picked up her Malbec and took a drink, inhaling some of the liquid in the process. Still holding the wine in her right hand, she coughed into the left, then took in a shuddering breath.

"Sorry. I think you startled me." Shaggy took another drink, more slowly this time. "I haven't, though I'm leaning toward an abortion."

"Did you want to talk about that?"

Those were almost the same words Moss had said to her, before she ran away. She felt so stupid. But she'd also known she couldn't stay.

Shaggy's phone buzzed on the table, rattling itself on the wood surface. Probably some late-night telemarketer. No else actually called. She flipped the phone over, intending to reject the call and block the number.

Bianca, her screen read.

"Shit. It's my mother. Must be an emergency. Excuse me?"

Laura waved a hand as if to say "of course," and went back to sipping at her wine.

"Hey Bianca." Shaggy picked up her own wine and took another drink. It was a good one, she finally noticed. Laura had picked out a smooth, rich, fruity vintage that was just the right amount of dry without the tongue-curling tannins Shaggy hated in a wine.

"Just hanging out with a friend. Doing some sewing. Talking. What's up?"

Shaggy tapped a nail against her glass, listening.

"No. I can't just come home next week. I have classes, and an order for a big show in early December that I need to plan for...and I'm busy with other stuff, too."

Bianca snorted in her ear, which just pissed Shaggy off. Her mother never believed Shaggy when she said she was busy. Shaggy knew she wasn't saving lives or something, but neither was Bianca. Just because her mother made more money didn't mean...

"Yes, the other stuff is important, Bianca. I don't know why you need me to impress the newspapers anyway. Aren't you enough? No, Mom. Damn it, Mom! No."

Shaggy's fingers curled around the bowl of the wine glass. She wanted nothing more than to hurl it across the room, to hear the shattering of glass and watch the spray of red on the white walls.

"I can't come, Mom. There's something I really need to deal with... What? *Yes*, it is important. I'm pregnant."

"Whoa," Laura said, setting her glass down and leaning forward, her smooth, unlined face all of a sudden creased with concern.

Shaggy hadn't planned on saying that to Bianca. Hadn't planned on telling her anything, in fact. But the words were out there now, and Shaggy couldn't take them back. Dammit. What the hell was she going to do now?

You'll have an abortion, of course. Bianca's words echoed in her ear.

"What did you say to me?" She barely recognized her voice. Barely recognized *herself*. Her fights with her mother were always a dance of passive aggression, never, ever direct confrontation. At least not on Shaggy's part.

Her mother's voice murmured in her ear, repeating the deadly words.

"What? Do you think I can't take care of a kid? No. You don't, do you? '*You can't even take care of your own life, Shaggy.*'" Her voice was harsh, pinched, mimicking and mocking. "That's what you would say, isn't it? That's what you think, isn't it? As though I didn't take care of myself and Dad all those years while you. Just. Fucked. Off."

Her mother spoke calmly in her ear. Shaggy barely heard the words.

"No. You don't get a say. Not now. And if you try to shut my trust down, I will fight you. Make no mistake. That money was Daddy's, too. And I deserve it for taking care of him when you wouldn't. No. No. Goodbye, Bianca. I'll talk to you later."

Shaggy mashed her thumb against her phone as hard as she could, cutting off the call, then threw the phone back down on the table. She scrubbed her hands across her face, then sat there, elbows on the table, head in hands, trying to catch her breath. Somewhere in the background, over the sound of her own beating heart, she heard Laura moving. Felt the woman standing next to her. Heard the sound of wine being poured. Then Laura sat next to her at the table, one hand on Shaggy's back.

"Here. Just take a sip. Then why don't we go sit on the couch, and you can tell me exactly what that bitch said."

Shaggy gave a small laugh and uncurled herself. She took the glass of wine from Laura's hands and drank.

"She just assumed I would have an abortion. Without even asking what I wanted, or what happened, or who the guy was, or if I was happy."

"Is she always that way?"

Shaggy rose and padded to the sofa. She plopped down on one end, and Laura folded herself onto the other. Both of them tucked their feet up.

Taking another drink of wine, Shaggy bought some time to think.

"You know, she wasn't always. When I was little, she was more...present, I guess. But then my dad started to go downhill and she retreated. Became more brittle. I think that was her way of coping, but I was still so young, you know?"

"It sounds shitty," Laura said. "Hard."

"It was. It really was. Sometimes I want to just get a job and say screw her money, but then I think I deserve it for... well, you heard."

"So, does this mean you want to keep the baby now? If that's the case, I should dump the rest of this very good wine down the sink."

Shaggy shook her head. "I don't think so. I really can't imagine having a kid. She just pissed me off so much. As if she even has a say. She doesn't."

Shaggy looked out the floor-to-ceiling windows, at the night. At the lights of the bridge and the cars crossing, east to west and back again, red lights. White lights. People.

Everyone living their own lives, with their own hopes and fears.

"I still have no idea what the right decision is, or if there is even a right decision, you know? All I know is that I want the decision to be *mine*."

13

MOSS

Moss arrived at the Inner Eye, heart racing, feeling as if he'd just run a marathon or been out in the streets facing cops all day. Brenda took one look, told him to make himself a cup of tea, and sent him to the little nook in the back end of the shop where she and a rotating group of psychics did readings for customers.

That's where he was now, sipping at one of Brenda's homemade rose petal and spearmint teas. Brenda had suggested chamomile, but despite its purported calming properties, he didn't like the taste of it. Just the act of inhaling the scent of this blend was enough to start calming him down. Or maybe it was the atmosphere in the shop.

The Inner Eye was a metaphysical shop of long standing, and Brenda and Tempest worked hard to keep the space energetically clean and clear. The reading nook was so psychically clean the air felt almost crisp inside the tiny space. The small alcove got cleared after each reading. He could smell the mingled scents of Florida Water spray, rosemary and mugwort smudge, and benzoin incense. Brenda had a variety of readers from different traditions, and they all used something different.

From the safety of the alcove, Moss's eyes scanned the bookshelves and the comfortable chairs where one customer sat leafing through a small stack of books on Jewish mysticism. Beyond that were display cases filled with statuary, crystals, stones, and magical tools. More shelves behind the front counter held jars filled with all sorts of supplies.

Moss felt his spirit relax, responding to the spirit of the store. It was a happy, well-fed spirit, and did a great job of protecting the space. No wonder he had run here. It wasn't just that he wanted Brenda's input, he realized; he needed to be around a kami that didn't feel disturbed.

In this space, his own troubled agitation was still present, but had its edges smoothed. He was still aware of the pain carried by the Willamette, and Shaggy's confusion —he still couldn't believe she'd run away like that—but they no longer pressed on him so hard. The sense of suffocation and panic had eased.

"Thank the Gods and Goddesses," he muttered, before blowing across the surface of his mug of tea and taking a long drink of the honey-sweetened brew. Unlike other members of Arrow and Crescent Coven, Moss wasn't dedicated to any particular deity, though he offered respect to them all. He wasn't sure yet if it was his mostly agnostic Buddhist upbringing, or the fact that he just hadn't yet met a deity who personally spoke to him, but he was fine with things the way they were. The kami kept him busy enough as it was. The forces of nature were vital and present in Portland, and the longer he worked with them and gave them offerings, the more alive the relationship became. Add in the kami of all the small things, plus taking care of his ancestors, and Moss wasn't sure where he'd find the time to establish a relationship with anything else.

Well, except maybe for Shaggy, if she decided she could actually talk to him about what was going on.

Speaking of relationships, he thought, here came his teacher. As she made her way through the aisles of her domain, he smiled. With glossy brown hair piled high on her head in an artful mess of loose curls, a flowing tunic the color of salmon, the silver bangles, drop earrings, and a giant moonstone at her breastbone, she looked like some sort of New Age royalty.

Moss supposed that she was, in a way. Her customers treated her with respect and reverence, and she'd been able to keep this shop not only open, but thriving, even as the street around her grew more expensive every year. No easy feat. The fact that she was a witch—and a lesbian—could have hurt her business, but instead, it only added to her mystique, lending her the power of people's imagination. Over the last couple of years of studying with Brenda and Raquel, Moss had come to learn that imagination was a potent thing.

"Better?" Brenda asked him, as she settled into the chair across from the small table.

Moss nodded.

"Ready to talk about it?"

He exhaled, then took another sip of tea. Brenda simply sat, graceful fingers laced together on the table, completely still, as if she didn't have a shop to run, employees to take care of, and a thousand other things to do. Moss wished he had an ounce of her ability to pay attention like that. Brenda would tell him to get back to his candle-gazing practice and develop his own power, rather than wishing he had hers.

"There's this woman…" He bit his lip. How to begin this? "And then there's the river…"

His right foot started bouncing under the table and his hands gripped the mug of tea.

"Shhhh," Brenda said, then reached out and made a tugging and flicking motion with her fingers near the top of his head, clearing away the thoughts that crowded, one after another, into his head. "Slow down."

He focused on slowly exhaling, then pausing, then slowly inhaling. Just the way Brenda had taught him.

"Open up your feet," she said. "And when you're ready, start with the woman."

Come on, Moss, this is basic, he thought with some disgust as he allowed his mentor to lead him through the exercises that should have been second nature by now. He felt his agitation recede. His shoulders dropped and he straightened his spine, sitting taller in his chair.

"There's this woman. Shaggy. We met at that festival I went to in August. Bliss. It was just supposed to be a fun hookup, you know? And now she's here. And she's pregnant. And she ran away after she told me today. And I don't know what to do."

He drank more tea and stared down at the table. He felt Brenda waiting for him to say more. He felt her willing him to look up. To face her. To face whatever this situation was. Damn it. He didn't want to.

If you didn't want to, you wouldn't have come here, his inner voice said.

Fuck you, he replied.

"What do you want?" Brenda asked. "Do you want a baby? Do you want to be with this woman?"

He looked at his mentor. He reached for the deep calm at her center, and the calmness of the Inner Eye. Then he tried to find his own center. It was there, but felt so small today.

"I want to do what's right, but its hard to know what that is, you know? And that's part of where the Willamette comes in. It's still being poisoned. We have to fight that *again*. How do I bring a baby into a world like this? But that feels like a cop-out, too. Do I tell Shaggy I'll get a real job? Something that actually pays? Give up the activism? What?"

He searched Brenda's face. Her eyes were so compassionate, but still, she just waited. Reflecting him back at himself. Waiting for him to figure himself out.

"But if I give up the activism, what kind of world does that leave for a kid?"

"And Shaggy? How do you feel about her? And what does she want?"

"I..." How *did* he feel about her? What was the truth? He dropped his attention into his core, trying to sense what was there, beneath the roiling swirl of emotion and thought. There it was, faint. A glimmer. Something real. "I'm really drawn to her. She's...special. But I don't think she knows that yet. She sells herself short. And it's funny, she's super rich or something. Like, if it weren't for EDM, we never would have met. So, on one hand, maybe she doesn't even need me. On the other hand, I want to do the responsible thing."

"And you think that means giving up activism and settling down into some sort of corporate job?"

"Well, not corporate maybe. But I could learn a trade or something. Maybe."

"I'm not saying that's a bad idea, Moss, but being a responsible adult doesn't mean giving up who you are. It means becoming more of who you are. When we are centered in ourselves, we understand our place in the community, and in the cosmos, and we can do our duty."

"Do our duty? That doesn't sound like fun."

"Call it something else then. Call it your True Will, like the Thelemites do. Or enacting your destiny."

"I still don't understand."

"Look at it this way...part of why the world is such a mess is that we, as a group and as individuals, are out of alignment. Out of true. Our souls are fractured, and this fractures our friend and family relationships, our communities, and the whole society."

Moss nodded. He felt the truth of Brenda's words inside his bones.

"So what do I do?" he asked her.

"Well, we should really do a course of shadow work, but that's going to need to wait. I want you to start practicing soul alignment, every single day. Throughout the day, in fact."

"And you think that's going to help?" Moss felt skeptical again. As though Brenda had turned into some white-lighter who thought humans could just pray their problems away.

"I know it will. Look, Moss, part of changing culture is changing ourselves. It's a long-term task, and trust me, I know how thankless that can feel, but we have to do it."

"Go live on a mountain?"

"No!" He'd never seen Brenda angry like this. "That is *not* what I'm saying at all. Stop acting like a wounded child and listen."

She paused and looked up. Tempest was waving her over to the counter where a customer needed some help.

"Excuse me," she said, rising from her chair. She stood there for a moment, piercing him with those blue eyes. "I've got to take care of this, but we have a lot more to talk about. For now, I'll just say that you have to stop looking at the world as black and white. It isn't, and if you would listen to the kami you work with, you would know that. Align your soul, Moss. You won't get any clarity otherwise."

Brenda strode off with a swirl of her tunic and a clash of silver bangles, leaving him to himself, and his thoughts, and the fact that Shaggy might not want any of this. She might not want him at all.

"Shit." And he hadn't even gotten to talking about the possible egregore. Would soul alignment help with that? Moss grabbed his messenger bag. He was sick of himself. Might as well go home. It was his week to clean the bathrooms anyway.

14

SHAGGY

The large, high-ceilinged black box of a room was a riot of activity, and smelled faintly of sweat, antiseptic, and chalk. Music blasted from the speakers while instructions and encouragement were shouted over the beat.

Shaggy had found a relatively quiet corner mat to stretch out on, eyes trained across the room where a man and a woman practiced on a trapeze, swinging out and back in tandem, flipping their bodies upside down, waiting for the big swing in which the smaller person would set themself free, fly through the air, and grasp their partner's forearms. It took Shaggy's breath away.

She heard a shout of laughter and the smack of hands on a mat from the opposite side of the room, where a tumbling class was in progress.

The teacher was a short, lightly muscled, trans woman named Monica. Apparently, she'd been a gymnast in middle and high school, had a sports scholarship to Portland University, and been slated for Olympic tryouts when she finally was able to come out as a woman. It was too complicated to go through hormones and switch teams at that point, she had told Shaggy over drinks one night, so Monica had dropped out. Gotten a job in a café. Worked for a while. Become the person she was always meant to be. Now she taught tumbling and coached gymnastics.

She said she was happy.

Despite having spent time down in the Bay around circus types, Shaggy was still in awe of these people. People like Monica—so sure of themselves, despite whatever bullshit life had thrown their way—made her examine her own self. Who was *she* supposed to be? Was she the responsible child, the caretaker who had to become an adult too quickly? Was she the free spirit, the trust fund kid, living off her mother's largesse and partying all the time? Was she a student, a designer, a budding aerialist...?

Or was she supposed to be a parent?

She had no idea. But for the first time in her life Shaggy really wanted an answer to that question.

"All warmed up? Ready to go?" Phoebe's voice came from her left, startling Shaggy. She hadn't even heard her trainer approach and looked up at the solid strength that was Phoebe, aerialist extraordinaire. Dark brown hair caught up in a loose bun at the base of her neck, thick roll of pale flesh sandwiched in between her purple bra tank and geometric patterned leggings, Phoebe was much curvier than Monica. Beneath the soft-looking flesh, Shaggy knew, were muscles hard as rocks. The woman was a tank.

Shaggy stood, stretched her arms over her head, and then swung them from side to side.

"Ready as I'll ever be," she replied.

She and Phoebe walked to another section of blue mats where long, pale swathes of silk dangled from the ceiling and puddled onto the floor. Shaggy stepped toward one of the silks, flexed her hands and feet, and then wound her hands in the fabric, reveling in the feel of it against her skin. She inhaled deeply, exhaling through her mouth, trying to calm the butterflies that had started up in her belly as soon as she began walking towards the aerial equipment. The butterflies were a combination of nervousness, fear, and excitement.

Standing on the mats, looking up at the twenty-foot ceiling, Shaggy was torn between the taste of freedom she got from the aerial work, and the fear that she would fall and snap a bone. Climbing the silks was always a risk, and that was part of what she liked about it.

And what sort of risks are you going to take with your life now? What are you going to choose?

She whisked the thought away, and focused on her breathing and the feel of fabric sliding through her palms. Phoebe stepped forward to anchor the silks as Shaggy climbed, winding her hands and feet in the silks, and jerking her way up and up, bit by bit. Her ascent wasn't very smooth yet, but her arms and shoulders had gotten a lot stronger since she'd started practicing again.

She'd begun studying the year before, down in San Francisco, and fallen in love. One of the first things she did when she moved to Portland was find this school, tucked behind a teal door on one of the side streets just off Hawthorne.

Fifteen feet from the floor now, Shaggy felt the moment Phoebe let go. The tension in the silks was up to her now. It was her job to keep things stable, and the only way to do that was to move her body into shapes she was barely beginning to understand.

Wrap the silks around each foot. Spread the arms. Bend to the left.

Form a triangle with the pelvis and legs. Bend to the right.

Climb your legs up the silks. Get ready. Let your hands go. Bend outward, reaching for the far wall, then soften. Allow your torso to reach toward the floor, until you are dangling upside down. Until you completely trust your own strength, and the strength of the fabric.

She could hear Phoebe's voice, calling out instruction from the silks just next to her, but she couldn't quite process the words. All the information was in her body. Her arms and legs, her torso and head, her pelvis and spine...they all knew just what to do.

Her body knew what her mind didn't seem to.

Dangling upside down, held suspended in the air, Shaggy began to cry. Not silent, pretty, tears slowly flowing from her eyes, but huge, silk-rocking sobs.

"Shaggy! Are you okay?" Phoebe's voice finally penetrated, but Shaggy didn't care.

Sobbing, snorting back tears and snot, she swung and rocked, and wound herself more tightly in the silks. She climbed upright again, and started the sequence over. Triangle. Reach. Bend. Flow.

This. This feeling was what she wanted. This thing she still couldn't name. She felt it in her muscles and her bones. She wanted this. This. This.

She wanted now. Every moment.

All of a sudden, Shaggy understood. There was no hiding. No running. There was simply being.

"Shaggy! Are. You. Okay. Do I need to get you down?"

Shaggy turned, finally, and saw Phoebe's worried face, five feet away, reaching out one arm.

She snorted back more tears, then laughed.

"Actually, I'm fine. Better than I have been in a long time."

Shaggy steadied her breathing once again, wiped her face on her shoulder, and started the routine again.

She still didn't know what she was going to do, but she knew she actually would be fine.

At least for now.

15
____

MOSS

Sunlight filtered through white sheers, warming up the old hardwood floors of Moss's bedroom. The big house was relatively quiet. Everyone else had already gone off to work, except for Maggie. She would be off to school soon though; he could hear her rattling around in the kitchen, the sounds of making coffee. She must have burned her toast again, because the charred scent had traveled upstairs through his door.

Moss's room was small, but comfortable. The space was just large enough for a double bed, a salvaged chest of drawers, and one small, comfy barrel chair that he'd picked up on the street. His favorite green comforter was pulled sloppily up over the bed, half over the pillows. Moss liked to keep his space neat, but he was also too lazy to make his bed properly, hence the comforter. It covered all manner of sins, including the fact that his sheets should have been thrown in the wash two days before.

He sat on the edge of the bed now, staring at his chest of drawers. It was a beautiful old walnut piece, one of those six-drawer jobs, but he wasn't actually staring at the dresser itself. His eyes were fixed on the space on top of it. His altar. A thin layer of dust covered the statues, brass candlesticks, and ritual objects. The thing really needed dusting, and rearranging, too.

Brenda was right, he needed to get back to basics. The less time a witch spent practicing their basic skills, the weaker their will became. And without a strong will? A witch's magic was nothing.

Will was harnessed intention. Whether a person wanted to hone the mind, calibrate the emotions, or train the body, developing will was required. And that was just the basic level of will. There was another thing that some magic workers called "True Will," and ever since Brenda had mentioned the *destiny* word, the magical concept had been ticking at the back of his brain.

Was activism his destiny? Was magic? Was being a parent?

What in the world was his True Will? And exactly how was he supposed to figure that out?

He was avoiding again, he realized. Rather than addressing the work at hand, his mind had drifted to a bigger picture he just couldn't see. Not right now. The larger philosophical and magical theories were just another way to avoid the fact that his altar was covered in the dust of neglect, and being busy wasn't a reason. It was just an excuse.

Moss needed to get his practice back on track. Without it, he would grow weaker and less focused. And the kami would stop talking to him altogether, their voices obscured by his own concerns. He knew that last one from long experience. The messages from the spirits and beings came through stronger the more centered and clear he was inside himself.

He needed a strong will for his activism work too. Throwing yourself in front of cops on a regular basis? That required a person to either be an adrenaline junkie, or have some great training for their fight or flight mechanism.

"Stop stalling," he said to the empty room. He stood and took two steps toward the chest of drawers. A beeswax candle waited in a brass candlestick, matches beside it. He definitely needed to clean the altar, but practice came first. Moss inhaled deeply, closing his eyes for a moment. He let his awareness trace the edges of his physical body, all the way down to his feet, then up his back and to the crown of his head. He wiggled his bare toes on the wood floor and flexed his fingers. Only then did he strike a match, inhaling the sulfur scent of it, and lit the taper. Waving the match out, he dropped it in a brass incense dish and picked up a short stick of cedar incense. He lit the tip, traced a pentacle shape over his altar, and placed the incense into the brass holder.

Drawing his hands up toward his face, he bowed, then poured water from his steel thermos into a pale green ceramic tea bowl that had once belonged to his grand-mother. The bowl connected him to his ancestors, and, as a witch, also to all of the powers of water.

Moss flexed his bare feet on the floor again, straightened his spine, and inhaled deeply. Then he clapped his hands three times, the sharp sound shattering the air.

"Great river, come to me. Flow through me. Be with me. Show me the ways of water, of sinking and swimming, of movement and reflection. Allow me to feel your depths, and revel in the power and lightness of your waves. May I be one with the creatures of the river. May I be one with your banks, and your sinuous curves. Great river, teach me how to honor you. Show me your way."

He bowed once more, then grabbed a meditation

cushion and sank down to the floor in front of the window next to his dresser altar, bathing in the mid-morning light.

Slowing his breathing down, he allowed his attention to drop into his belly like a stone falling into a deep pool. He softened the focus of his eyes, and felt his shoulders drop and sink into place.

Moss breathed, smelling the sweet, clean musk of the cedar, and the rich honey notes of melting beeswax.

Images darted through his mind like schools of fish. Shaggy's face, lit by sunshine. The strobe lights of the dance club. The river. Images of himself, arms in long tubes, locked down to his comrades. Police in riot gear. Shaggy again, eyebrows creased with worry. Cormorants skimming over the water.

He inhaled again, more slowly and deeply, trying not to clutch at the thoughts.

Trying to flow like the river itself.

::*Stop trying.*::

The message came as more of a sense inside of himself than a voice in his ears. Moss's psychic skill was clairsentience, the knowing of things through the body. Brenda said that was why he was so good at tuning into the spirits of place—his body felt the connection with the spirits that dwelled in all things.

Are you the river?

::*Does it matter?*::

Moss returned to his breath, and imagined the edges of his body opening and relaxing. Allowing his attention to move outward, he imagined his etheric body and his aura also softening.

Be like water. He smiled, then returned once again to his breath.

The images floating by changed. Herons. Bitterns.

Egrets. Osprey. Chinook. Trout. Sturgeon. Crappie. Bass. Feathers and scales, flying and swimming.

His breathing deepened, and so did his consciousness. The river flowed on.

Cottonwood. Willow. Maple. Hemlock. Ash. Lichen and moss.

And deeper still. Pain. Suffocation. Copper. Acid. Ammonia. The stink and sting of chemicals not native to the water itself. The struggle of the animals and fish.

No matter how fast the river ran, it could not clean itself. And something was making sure of that.

::Help me, and I shall teach you all the ways of water.::

Moss floated, skin stinging. Lungs on fire, he began to swim.

Show me.

The river led him to a space beneath the gothic towers of St. John's Bridge. Deeper and deeper he swam, until he was almost at the riverbed, down in the mucky sludge beneath the piers.

And there it was. The source of the disease. The cancer infecting the river. The taste of oil-slicked rainfall. The stink of car exhaust and coal. The waste of ten thousand container ships. The bite of ammonia.

Blood from the core of the earth, pumped up from its heart to be consumed, and then discarded, burned, and dumped as if it were not precious.

::Out of place.::

I know.

Moss's consciousness opened to the river, and to the toxic sting of benzo(a)pyrene, ammonia, and other chemicals on his skin. He felt the suffocation of the plant life, and the heaviness slicking feathers and choking scales.

It was simply out of place, having been stolen with no

way to put it back. Someone had taken the out-of-placeness and manipulated it into something more. Something trying to burrow deeper. Make a home where no home should be.

But how do we put this to rights? he thought.

::Bring back the flow.::

Moss swam upward then, so slowly, level by level, layer by layer, he rose up toward the river's surface, and to waking consciousness. His eyes blinked at the morning sun. The scents of cedar and beeswax replaced the stink of chemicals and oil.

He still had no idea what the river meant, but he could feel the sense of it in his soul. He had to become like water. He had to flow like the river.

That truth would set him free.

16

SHAGGY

The doctor's office was about as cozy as you would expect. Shaggy sat in a crinkly paper robe on the crinkly paper examining table cover swinging her legs, and waiting. You always had to wait for doctors, even if they were just nurse practitioners and not really doctors at all.

Her stomach was filled with butterflies again, and not the good kind, the kind that made her feel half-queasy even though all she'd had for breakfast was a piece of peanut butter toast and a cup of milky tea.

And the need to run was back, along with the image of Moss's face when she had left the café. That was a shitty thing to do, and she knew it, but she couldn't have done anything else. Maybe she'd text him. Apologize. Ask to see him again.

Did she want to see him again? The question made her stomach lurch. She swallowed, hard. She was not going to puke again. She was tired of puking, and was growing tired of the indecision, too. Not that her bouts of self-loathing were helping anything.

Fluorescent lights hummed overhead. Cheerful posters

detailed human anatomy. Equally cheery racks of pamphlets detailed sexually transmitted illnesses and how to beat urinary tract infections. There was the standard tiny hand-washing sink. A computer with a rolling stool sat in front of it. Shaggy should have kept her phone with her. Distracted herself by scrolling social media, or playing one of her dumb, pattern-matching games. But as soon as she got up from the paper covered exam table to fish it out of her purse, the nurse practitioner would walk in, she knew it.

But she couldn't sit here with her thoughts anymore, either. Shaggy sighed, and scooted forward enough to get her dangling feet to the cold, tiled floor. Sure enough, that instant, the tap came at the door, followed by the sound of the knob turning.

"Sarah Richter?"

"That's me," Shaggy replied.

The nurse practitioner came over and shook her hand. She barely looked older than Shaggy, and wore cute, pink-framed glasses perched on a pert nose. Her blond hair was slicked back in a utilitarian bun, but those glasses said it all, as did the pink lipstick on the woman's smiling lips. Nurse Practitioner Swenson was one fun chick.

"Before I start the exam, do you have any questions?"

Shaggy shifted on the crinkly paper.

"How far along can you be before the pills won't work?"

The woman paused, then went to the sink to wash her hands. "Did you do a home test, or come in for testing?"

"Home test."

After a thorough scrubbing, NP Swenson pumped out two paper towels from the wall machine using her elbow. Drying her hands, she turned. "Well, we should do an exam to make sure, but how long has it been since your last period?"

"Around seven weeks," Shaggy replied. She'd been thankful for that, she remembered. Her period was never reliable, and she'd been happy to not be heading to the festival with cramps. Her doctor in California had bugged her to go back on the pill to help with her symptoms, but the pills made Shaggy feel bloated and lethargic, and she hated feeling that way. And since she didn't need them for birth control—or so she thought—a random period and bad cramps every two to three months seemed like a small price to pay.

"You're in luck. Mifepristone and misoprostol work up until twelve weeks, although many people find a D&C a lot less taxing on the body. But I see here on your chart you've had irregular periods and suffer from endometriosis." The space between NP Swenson's eyebrows creased. "What made you think you were pregnant?"

Hoo boy. How was Shaggy going to explain this? She shifted on the exam table, the paper crinkling beneath her. Her feet were cold, her palms were sweating, and she really wished she'd kept her socks on. She wanted out. Out of the antiseptic smell, away from the crinkling paper and the cold, and out from under this woman's stare.

"I just had a sense..." she started, then stopped again, unsure how to proceed. "Over the years, I've gotten pretty used to things feeling weird down there. I know it's too soon...but something just seemed off. And then a few days ago, I started to feel nauseated. Even the smell of coffee made me queasy. So I got a home test."

What Shaggy couldn't tell NP Swenson was that she'd always gotten weird intuitive hits, and even messages some-times. It was part of why she knew she had to take care of her father. She knew she'd never be able to live with herself if she hadn't. He needed her help to set some things in order in his soul before he died. Shaggy never talked to anyone about that stuff. Bianca rolled her eyes at the merest hint of "woo" as she called it, so Shaggy had learned to keep things to herself.

"And you're sure you don't want to keep it? You do know that with your condition..."

"I know. And no. I haven't one-hundred percent decided yet. But I wanted to see what my options were."

"Sounds good. Let's get started with this exam then."

NP Swenson pulled the metal stirrups out from the bottom of the table, and Shaggy scooted herself into position, bracing for the cold metal of the speculum.

Whether she would let this embryo grow into something more, she still didn't know, but it was a relief to have a choice.

17

MOSS

He sat in another classic old Portland building with a high, vaulted ceiling, but this time, instead of dancing in a moving throng, Moss was wedged into an uncomfortable wooden chair, sitting next to the few coven members who had managed to make the meeting, plus a bunch of other activists he'd worked with off and on for years.

They were all people he would trust with his life, which was a good thing. He didn't want to go into an action like this without that basic sense of trust.

The room smelled of sweat, spearmint gum, and the papery scent of the ghosts of a thousand union members, pressed into the walls.

A union hall in Southeast Portland might have seemed like a strange place to be meeting, but it had hosted a whole array of radical meetings in its day. Moss and the coven took up half a row of chairs on the floor. Members of the Clean Rivers Coalition had called the meeting after some strategic phone calls from Moss and Terra had alerted them to the news of a possible new polluter in their midst. An environmental science student had tested the waters and sure enough, along with the usual levels of mercury and PCBs—polychlorinated biphenyls—that made it unsafe to eat fish from the rivers, there were increased ammonia, benzo(a)pyrene and Polycyclic aromatic hydrocarbons (PAHs) levels in the water.

It was exactly what the river had told Moss.

The usual cohort of anarchists, socialists, and environmentalists were threaded through with the St. John's Neighborhood Project, the Interfaith Community for Justice, and members of the American Indian Movement. A small cadre of Brown Berets stood in the back of the room, talking with members of Families for Black Lives.

The radical left wasn't always good at getting along, but when a group made up largely of First Nations activists called a meeting, folks showed. The events at Standing Rock had galvanized a lot of people, and made the connections between environmental injustice, racism, and the class divide crystal clear. The consistent polluting of the Willamette, despite decades of effort to clean it up, was a direct threat to poor people, and to the Black and indigenous peoples of Portland and beyond.

A bunch of people were still researching their target—they needed solid evidence since they couldn't go on Moss's hearsay. A series of actions was likely in their future, but for now, the insult to the river wouldn't stand. Whoever it was, was going to pay, if not in dollars, at least in public embarrassment and with a lot of harassment.

So far, most of the research had thrown shade on a huge waste disposal company based in Washington state, called GranCo. Alejandro would neither confirm nor deny, but a press conference was coming up with the company, and Moss intended to be on site, just in case.

Kiyiya stood next to a wooden podium on the stage at the front of the big hall, microphone in hand, bottle of water at the ready. An older man with short, salt-and pepper hair and soft dark eyes, he wore a Pendleton plaid shirt, jeans, and boots. A long-time fixture in AIM since its inception in the 1960s, he'd also been a union member when he was young, if Moss recalled right. These days he devoted all of his time to his grandchildren and activism.

"Thank you all for coming," he said, his voice a low rumble, his cadence as fluid as a song. "As Henrietta said in her beautiful prayer, we are here because water is life, and the Great Creator has blessed us with these two beautiful rivers that are the lifeblood of our people."

He took a sip of water from his bottle, and cleared his throat.

"You know that we have a celebration of the waters planned for Saturday. The blessing ceremony will continue, but the friends and allies of the river, and the creatures of the river, of the salmon, and the cormorants, and all of those who rely upon the waters, will gather to fight."

The elder's soft, dark eyes swept over the crowd gathered in the union hall. How a man could be so soft and yet so powerful? It was something Moss could barely fathom, but he felt the *truth* of it in his bones. Brenda and Raquel both had those qualities, too. He hoped he might become that way someday. Maybe he could soften to what was real, and fight for what was true. Whether that ended up being the land, a child of his own, or the children of his friends and comrades, it didn't matter. All of it was sacred. All of it mattered.

"The great John Trudell said, 'They pollute the air, they pollute the water, they pollute our food, they pollute our minds.' He also told us we must resist. Fight back. Well, a lot of us have been fighting back for a long time, and we're not going to stop. The EPA says it will not pay to clean our river anymore, that the polluters must pay. It is our job to remind the government and these polluters that just because they have money and guns, doesn't mean we don't have power."

Kiyiya's gaze held Moss's just for a moment, before moving on. "We have the power given to us by the land, the sky, and the waters. We are one with the salmon and the cormorant who rely on clean water. Our children rely on clean water. Water is life. I say these words to remind us all that no matter what we do this Saturday, we do it to honor the water. We are part of this land and that is the truth we must constantly reveal. Our job is not to just expose the corruption of these filthy corporations. If that is all we do, we fail. Our job is to remind the people that we are of this earth and water, and that without this connection, life itself will cease to be."

Kiyiya stopped speaking, but no one stepped up to fill the void. Moss felt the energy of the room, and the spirit of the people, as that spirit soaked in the elder's words.

Saturday was the equinox. The balance of night and day, dark and light. Moss could feel that, too. If he centered himself deeply enough, and stilled the clamoring inside, he could almost feel the axial tilt, the inexorable lengthening of the earth's shadow meeting the light of the sun.

Then Terra took the mic. "Thank you, Kiyiya. Your words honor us. As we plan tonight, I hope we all keep them in mind. Okay. The Clean Rivers Coalition and the Yakama and Chinook elders have asked us to do a series of actions centered around Saturday's ceremony, but first, I'd like you all to power down your phones and computers. And don't speak of any but the most strictly legal actions in this room. If your affinity group wants to bend the rules? Discuss that in a safe space, and make sure that you know everyone in the room with you."

There was a rustling and creaking as people moved to comply. Moss powered his own phone all the way down. It wasn't enough. There were probably agents in the crowd, as there always were, but security protocol was security protocol. Hence Terra's warning. That was as much of a reminder as Kiyiya's words.

"Thank you," Terra said. "We're taping up time sheets on the walls in the back. If your affinity group has something particular in mind, please sign up for a time slot. If you don't have an affinity group, don't worry. Some groups have space for people to join in on some pretty fun, effective projects. Some only require the ability to make a sign with targeted messaging, others, I hear, may require costumes."

Terra smiled at that, and there were chuckles throughout the room.

Moss knew what he would be doing, and it wasn't something that could be discussed in an open forum.

It was just the sort of risk he lived for. And maybe Brenda was right. Maybe this was what being an adult looked like. And maybe it was part of his destiny.

18

SHAGGY

Shaggy had spent the evening working on clothing designs while waiting for Moss to show up. She'd finally texted him after her doctor's appointment, apologizing and asking if he still wanted to talk. He said he would be late because of some sort of activist meeting, but that he would show up.

Well, Moss was here now, and her sewing sat abandoned, the small dining table off the kitchen strewn with fabrics and the trusty sewing machine.

Moss and Shaggy sat on opposite ends of the rust velvet sofa, two bookends staring at the low gas flames flickering in the white-tiled fireplace. It wasn't really cool enough outside for a fire, but Shaggy wanted the comfort of it. Moss ate his way through the chocolate cookies she'd set out. She'd had a few herself because they seemed to settle her stomach. She just wished the ginger mint tea would do its thing and settle her nerves.

"The doctor said there's still time to take the pills."

"And what does that look like?"

Shaggy shrugged, discomfort crawling over her skin. "It

means the thing is just a mass of tissue at this point and I can self-abort. It sounds pretty unpleasant—painful even—but then it'll be done."

"Like a miscarriage?"

She nodded, then stared at the flames. The conversation was the right thing, she'd decided, but that didn't mean she wanted to be having it.

"She said a D&C would be faster and easier on the body. So, there's that, too."

"So, what are you going to do? What do you think you want now?" he asked, face screwed up with concern, cookie in one hand and tea mug in the other.

Tonight, Moss wore a big gray knitted cowl over a long-sleeved T-shirt and looked pretty enough to eat, if she was so inclined. Part of her wanted to crawl across the couch, lay her head in his lap, and let him stroke her short hair. The other part wanted him out of her space so she could curl up in bed with the stack of novels loaded onto her e-reader.

That impulse to escape was still there, too. To take the damn abortion pills, buy an RV, and either join a circus for real, or hit the festival circuit. She'd looked into it and there were still plenty of shows in the warmer states to keep her occupied for the next couple of months, at least. And that might buy her enough time to figure out what she wanted from life.

"Do you want a kid?" he was saying. "Because if you do, we'll figure it out. I mean, you can figure out how much you want me around, what kind of parenting arrangements we need to make..."

"Moss." Shaggy set her mug down on the coffee table and waved her hands. "Stop. You're not responsible for this. I only let you know because..."

Why had she told him? This one-weekend-stand, festival guy who clearly didn't have two nickels to rub together?

"Because why?" He clutched his mug in both hands now, cookies gone. She could see the hurt in his eyes and wasn't sure if she cared. It was her life, after all. And she was the one who was going to have to deal with the consequences either way. Moss? Sure, he was talking like he was a stand-up guy, but the reality was, she didn't know him. Not one bit.

"Because I ran into you, I guess."

His head snapped as if she'd struck him and she wished she could take the words back, snatch them from the air and shove them back into her mouth. But she couldn't.

"I'm sorry, Moss. I'm just confused. I've spent the past six years planning my life around the fact that I can't have kids and now, to be pregnant? I feel like I should want a kid, but I can't really say that I do."

He exhaled with what might have been relief, might have been something else.

"If you want to have an abortion, I'll support you, of course. And look, I get that I'm just some hookup, but I also really clicked with you, Shaggy. I *like* you. And I'd like to get to know you, kid or no."

He still looked stricken, and so vulnerable. Open. She couldn't bear to look at his face, afraid of what might happen if she stared at him one more second.

Shaggy picked up her mug and padded into the kitchen to fill the kettle. The kitchen space was only a couple of dozen feet from the sofa, but at least it was a separation. She clicked the kettle on, the little handle glowing blue to indicate it was working. But she still didn't turn around.

"Do *you* want kids?" she asked softly. Waiting.

He was silent, and she finally looked over at him, to see if he had heard. He was leaning over the back of the velvet sofa, chin on his forearms, staring out the big windows at her favorite view. The lights on the bridges, reflecting on the Willamette. The red and white car lights, going and coming.

"I don't know if I want them or not," he finally replied, still staring outside. "I mean, I'm not exactly set up for it. And don't know if I want to raise a kid in this world. It feels too hard. Harsh."

The kettle binged softly, telling Shaggy the water had boiled.

"More tea?"

"Sure." Moss sighed, picked up his cup, and joined her in the small kitchen. "And you still haven't answered my question."

"You didn't ask me a question." An evasion, that was for sure. Something she had learned from dealing with Bianca.

"You know what I mean. Do you want me around? Kid or no?"

She finally looked him in the eyes, for the first time that night. She liked his eyes. Liked his whole face, as a matter of fact.

"I don't know anything right now, Moss. I barely know who I am, which sucks, because I felt like I finally had a chance to figure that out, and then, this, you know?" She fished two teabags from the canister on the counter and poured more water into both mugs. "Can we talk about something else for a while? I just...my head isn't clear."

"Sure," he replied. "My head isn't exactly clear, either."

Huh. That was interesting. She really didn't know what to do with someone who actually listened to her. Who didn't push, or grow impatient and angry, or run away. Or die.

"So," she said, once they were settled on the couch again, sipping at their tea, "what was your meeting about tonight?"

"The river," he said, gesturing toward the windows. "The Willamette."

"What about it?"

He exhaled sharply, then took a sip of tea. "Where to start? It's been polluted for a century, with all sorts of shit dumped in it. Runoff from mines. Oil. Sewage. Chemicals."

"And no one's ever tried to clean it up?"

"Oh yeah. Parts of the river have been superfund sites for a couple of decades now. Problem is, that's really expensive, the river's still polluted, and they don't want to pay anymore. Also, there's a new polluter out there...." He looked down at his mug, brow creased, then back at her. His face, so open before, looked hard now. Determined. "And whoever they are, I really want to take them down. And if I can't take them down, I at least want to make their lives really fucking uncomfortable. And even if it isn't someone new, the companies who've been profiting from dumping, and runoff, and burning shit in the air that ends up sinking into the water? They need to pay."

His voice grew louder the more he talked, the hand not holding his tea mug waving in animated arcs. Moss looked fierce. Determined. Passionate. She could see why he was an activist, with passion like that.

She didn't feel passionate about anything. For so long, she didn't have the time, and now that she had the time...

Shaggy cared about the environment, but only in some abstract, recycling-is-good kind of way. She'd been to festivals that raised money for various causes, but frankly there'd been too much on her plate dealing with her dad to pay attention. He hadn't been gone long enough for her to get used to having any choices at all.

"How are you going to do that? Hold them accountable, I mean?"

He shrugged, and drank some more tea. "We're planning some actions, like we always do. It won't be enough, because it never is, at least at first. But we've had some victories, you know. It's just, we never seem to get time to celebrate because there's always something new trying to keep the people down."

Shaggy shook her head. "Do you really think that's true?"

"Look, I said I like you, Shaggy, and I mean that. I want to get to know you better. I'd love to roll around in bed with you again if you're up for it. I wouldn't even mind having a kid with you, maybe, even though that scares the shit out of me...."

Her lips compressed, trying to hold back words. The longer he spoke, the more she wanted to lash out.

"But you think I'm just some spoiled rich girl who doesn't care about anything outside herself."

Fuck him and everyone like him.

"No. That's not what I said. I just..."

"You just what?"

He smacked his mug onto the coffee table and stood up in a rush, running his hands through his black hair.

"Look," he said, pacing between the sofa and the kitchen, "I just have a hard time talking to non-activists about this stuff sometimes. It isn't you. It's that," he threw his hands up in frustration, "most people don't take it seriously. Not unless they're already involved."

"So involve me, then." The words were a challenge, hanging in the air. Moss stopped and turned.

Shaggy wondered which of them looked more surprised. Him? Or her?

19

MOSS

The streets of the Pearl were thinning out by the time Moss left Shaggy's place. The night was chilly, and he was glad for his hand-knit cowl and long sleeves. He walked past shuttered cafés and specialty shops, skirting past people exiting a couple of bars.

It wasn't closing time yet, but, being a weeknight and all, people with regular day jobs were trundling off to bed, leaving the service workers to close out and clean up. He knew some of *them* might not get to bed until the office drones were getting out of bed again.

After the little flare-up, Moss and Shaggy had talked for two more hours, about environmentalism, the river, and a little bit about the action coming up. She had actually seemed interested, which was cool.

The thing they didn't talk about again was the two of them, or the pregnancy, even when she'd broken out a bottle of wine. He'd bit his tongue about that one. Her body, her choice, right? Though it did point toward the whole "getting rid of the zygote" thing. Regardless, the fact that she wouldn't talk about it ate at him a little. He'd been all prepared to do the right thing, to be the strong, supportive guy, but she'd shut the conversation down.

He supposed he couldn't blame her, but had to admit he felt pretty confused about it all. First of all, despite the fact that she *was* a bit of a rich princess, he liked her. Second of all, weren't women supposed to be the ones wanting to discuss everything?

"Where'd that bit of sexist bullshit come from, dickhead?" he said to the night air.

"Excuse me?" said a man who had just stepped out from Lumberjacks, a bar that Moss had actually been to on occasion. The man outweighed Moss by at least fifty pounds, and had a scowl on his face.

Shit. He hadn't even realized he'd said the words aloud.

"Sorry," Moss replied, "just talking to myself."

The man paused, staring, then gave a curt nod and swung by Moss. Thankfully, he was heading the opposite direction.

Moss exhaled, and kept walking.

He knew he should be relieved about the whole "we're not talking about the pregnancy now" thing, because it meant he could focus all of his attention on the equinox. To do an action like the one coming up, he needed to prepare inside. His affinity group was well trained, and had done this sort of thing several times, but every one of them was a cascade of adrenaline, righteous anger, and fear.

But the stakes had never felt higher, which was a little messed up, if he thought about it. Why did it matter so much if it was his child, instead of someone else's? It shouldn't, and he knew it, but there it was.

He crossed the street toward his car. Was there something on his windshield? Wait.

"Shit."

A huge crack spiderwebbed across his windshield. He wasn't even sure he'd be able to drive the thing. Damn it.

He hurried closer, heart pumping in his chest. Beneath the windshield wiper, a piece of white paper was neatly folded. Before he could even think, he ripped it from beneath the rubber blade, leaving one corner behind. It felt weird in his fingertips. Not like magic exactly, but...

Moss unfolded the paper and stared at the glued on letters from a magazine. *What the—?*

STay AwaY FRoM the riVer.

"Are you kidding me?"

His head whipped around, as if he was going to see some menacing figure smoking a cigarette in a doorway nearby. There was no one.

"Damn it!" He smacked his fist into the paper, crumpling it. "Damn it, damn it, *damn* it!"

He went back to his poor little car. The windshield was a mess, but it wasn't as bad as he feared. One large crack ran from the top of the driver's side, sloping down and across, with the worst of the spiderwebbed cracks on the passenger's side. He would be able to see to drive the thing home at least, but he wouldn't be able to pick up passengers in a car that looked like this, plus, it was probably not legal.

Not that Moss cared too much about legal, but he needed to keep his driver's license.

What the hell was he going to do now? Alejandro. He would know what to do.

He pulled out his phone and dialed.

"Hey, brother. I know it's late but...someone just smashed my windshield and threatened me. And my phone's been acting up lately. Makes me wonder if something's up with that, too. Yeah, the battery's been draining too quickly.... I got it six months ago. Right. And I've gotten some weirder-than-usual robo calls. And spam texts that don't seem quite right. But, yeah. A threatening note. Cracked windshield. Also, I think there might be an egregore at play or something. I can't quite tell."

Alejandro said he'd text the rest of the coven. They needed to meet anyway, to decide what part of the equinox action they were going to take on.

"Thanks, brother. Yeah, I'm good to get home. Talk to you tomorrow."

Moss stood on the sidewalk and stared at his windshield as if the spiderweb cracks held some message he wasn't seeing yet. Maybe he needed to tap into the kami of the windshield. He snorted at himself. It wasn't that glass wouldn't have a spirit, but something mass-manufactured held less and less of its original essence and became a very difficult thing to tap. Oh, maybe if Moss was some sort of master he could talk to his windshield, but he was nowhere near that. His own mentors had told him to go back to the beginning, and even the river had instructed him in the most basic precept: flow. So yeah, he was as far from mastery right now as he'd been for a long while.

He uncrumpled the paper and stared back down at the pasted-down words.

STay AwaY FRoM the riVer.

"I'm not going to do that, you fuckers. This river is part of the city, and so am I. I'm going to be like water, and you are going to drown."

Master or not, he'd make good on that promise.

20

SHAGGY

Blue silk wrapped around and around her thighs, which were bare beneath Spandex shorts, trailing past her calves down toward the floor. A material so soft and pliable, yet here it was, supporting her body twenty feet in the air.

She was still rusty, but every time she was back on the silks, her body remembered.

Right knee bent beneath her, she extended her left leg straight behind, flexing the muscles, feeling the silk adjust itself around her, bearing her weight. She pointed her toes and, right arm gripping the tower of silk, she arched her back, and brought her left arm over her head in a graceful curve, carving an arc in the surrounding space.

The black box of a room was deserted this early in the day. Blue mats opened beneath her, ready to cushion her body if she fell. One of her favorite artists, Autre ne Veut, filled the room with a moody, synth-backed combination of electronics and R&B.

Her body moved to the rolling beats as her heart and mind sank into Arthur Ashin's high falsetto, following his voice like a river. She was nothing but this, a heart in a chest, lungs filling with air, muscles reaching for something just beyond her grasp.

Supported by one of the lightest fabrics in the world.

"Get ready to roll!" Phoebe's voice burst through the music and Shaggy tensed, just for a moment, before breathing through the music once again.

Roll. She hadn't practiced rolls in almost a year. Her stomach fluttered at the thought of the drop, but her body also remembered there was nothing like the sensation of suspension, and free fall, and the great, jerking force that meant the silks still held her, safe above the ground.

"Shaggy?"

"Ready," she called down.

Shaggy inhaled as deeply as she could, trying to soothe the tremor in her belly. She knew she just had to get back on the horse, as it were. There was no way to prepare for a roll, except to roll. She stabilized again, both hands on the silk, and closed her eyes. She felt the vibrations of music move around and through her. She grabbed ahold of the music and let the music grab a hold of her.

And then she let go.

Her body flipped and arced and tumbled through space. With a swoosh, the silk tightened and loosened, then slid and gripped her thighs as it held her, then unwound. Held. Unwound. Slid, then gripped. Shaggy tumbled, free falling down, until her body stopped, jerked up briefly, then settled back into the cradle of silk.

She dangled, hands and head down, just five feet from the blue mats below. Hands grasping the swathes of silk again, she gently swung her body back-and-forth. Moving in time with the music, she threw both of her legs outward in a large, upside-down V and lifted her arms straight out, shoulders supporting biceps, supporting elbows, supporting forearms, supporting hands.

She spun there as the silks unwound themselves and slowly, so slowly, she allowed herself to slide down to the floor. Both palms flat on the mats, Shaggy softened for just a moment before lowering herself all the way down to the floor. The silks puddled around her head as she lay face up on the mats, staring upward into the sweep of the blue that reached towards the pitch black ceiling. She was sweating, and breathing in short gasps. Her body felt warm and alive. This was it, this was what freedom felt like. And she wanted it again, and again.

It felt good to know what she wanted, even if it was only for a few minutes.

Phoebe sat down on the mat beside her, boneless. Maybe someday Shaggy would have the strength and flexibility of the larger woman, but for now she just felt damn pleased with what she did have.

"You did great," Phoebe said, pulling her brown hair into a ponytail. "It seems like you're getting your old skills back pretty quickly. Your body is remembering, just like I said it would."

"It feels so *good*," Shaggy replied. "I'd almost forgotten how good it felt."

"Well, welcome back. Pretty soon we'll have you suspending from trees in the middle of festivals, or dropping from St. John's Bridge."

A frisson of heat raced through Shaggy's body, lighting up her skin.

"Why did you say that?"

"Oh, it's just a thing we Portland aerialists always talk about. Who doesn't want to suspend from the most gorgeous bridge in town?"

Shaggy rolled onto her side and pushed up into a seated position. Phoebe gave her a curious look, then turned. Once both women faced each other, Phoebe asked, "What's up?"

"How much do you know about the river?"

"The Willamette? The river that divides Southeast from Southwest? The one that the dragon boats race on, the one where they periodically kill seals who are eating the salmon?"

"Yeah." Shaggy smirked. "The Willamette."

Phoebe nodded. "What about it?"

Shaggy's heart was beating in her throat. This felt important, though she couldn't have articulated why.

"Well...I'm not sure how much I'm supposed to say about it, but there's a big action being planned...."

21

MOSS

The wind whipped off the river, smelling slightly of fish and mud. Moss shivered, drawing the knit cowl over his head for protection. He was glad for the light jacket he'd thrown over his long-sleeved T-shirt, too. Autumn was closing in quick.

He was clustered with Tariq, Kiyiya, and some other activists from the Clean Rivers Coalition. They stood out in the cold, late summer, pre-autumn breeze because Alejandro had just happened to text Moss a link to GranCo's website, with the word "Alert" followed by a "sorry, meant to send that to someone else." As if. Alejandro was just covering his ass regarding the NDA he'd signed, Moss was sure.

When Moss clicked on the web page there was an announcement. GranCo had called a press conference. The announcement—more of a press release—definitely sang the praises of this "alternative energy for the Pacific North-west" company. Anytime a corporation wanted to crow about themselves, activists became suspicious enough to pay attention. It was pretty clear something was up.

Besides which, Moss just had a bad feeling about all this. His bad feeling was confirmed by the fact that his coven brother Alejandro stood off to one side, removed from the cluster of suits, earbuds in, talking softly to someone on his phone. Every once in a while Alejandro would glance up at Moss and shake his head.

Yep, it really didn't look good. He was glad he'd called in reinforcements to witness whatever this farce turned out to be.

Standing on the edge of Cathedral Hill Park, his growing unease increased, shifting toward a sense of menace. It really did have the feel of an egregore to Moss, though he had no proof of that yet, either.

He squinted in the sun, waiting for the damn event to start. It was a small crowd, but packed with local heavy hitters. Even the mayor was out here. Asshole. Moss couldn't understand why the guy was still in office, not after Arrow and Crescent had revealed his collusion with corrupt land developers who'd been setting fires throughout the city to collect on insurance. Just goes to show you how much shit liberals were willing to put up with just to make a few more bucks.

A white woman in a skirt suit, dark hair slicked back into a bun, stray strands barely touched by the stiff breeze, stepped forward. As she strode toward a bristling clutch of TV microphones, she smiled, teeth blinding and eyes almost washed out in the sun reflected off the river. Print and radio reporters rushed forward to set their small rigs on the ground, or gathered close, holding recorders in outstretched hands.

Looking at her, Moss felt the way he had when he touched the paper stuck to his windshield, but he couldn't figure out why. Was she connected to the sense of menace? Or was he just having a knee-jerk reaction to what looked like another mover and shaker in a suit?

Speaking of...a white man in a gray suit flanked her, standing at parade rest, which was interesting. Was he a bodyguard or another exec? Moss didn't see a coiling ear wire, and the suit frankly looked too expensive for a flunky, no matter how well paid. The man shifted, adjusting his cuffs, and the bright wink of a Rolex caught the sun. Yep. Must be another exec.

"Greetings! Thank you all for joining us today." The woman's too-bright gaze scanned the reporters, then fell upon the small group of activists. Her mouth and eyes tightened, just for an instant, before she smoothed herself out again. "I'm Patricia Sloane, Environmental Engineer of GranCo, and I'm here today with Bradley Titus, CEO. In other words, my boss."

She grinned widely, expecting laughter that never came.

"Probably used to working a boardroom," Tariq muttered.

The boss. But she was no flunky, that was for sure.

"We're here to talk about the great plans we have for this great river, and this great city."

"Good Gods, who wrote her script?" Moss muttered back.

And how the hell had Alejandro ever considered working for these assholes?

"GranCo has worked with several cities in Washington state, installing state-of-the-art filtration systems in their water treatment plants. Our filtration is proven to reduce the risk of waste products and spillage, protecting the great waterways of the Pacific Northwest. As you may know, we also provide electricity to several counties in Washington through our waste disposal plants. In other words, we take your trash and, rather than shipping it off to landfill, use it to keep your lights on."

Moss felt the river whispering in his blood. The pressure inside of him built until it was almost painful to not speak.

Wait for questions. Wait for questions. Wait for questions. The litany built along with the pressure, as Moss tried to control the urgency, and dam the kami, that wanted him to speak *now*.

"GranCo is proud to announce that we signed a contract with the city of Portland six months ago and already the Willamette is cleaner than it's ever been! We're working with the city on the possibility of using our trash to power systems, as well..."

Inside Moss's heart, a dam broke.

"That's a lie!" he shouted. "The river is *more* polluted now! And what about the air?"

The smile froze on Patricia Sloane's face, and the reporter's heads swiveled his way. Moss saw the flash of a grin from Alejandro, quickly gone, as he shoved his phone in his pocket.

"As I said, our state-of-the-art..."

"This river is only as clean as it is because of this group of activists, here! Especially our comrades from the Yakama and Chinook nations!" Tariq yelled so loud, the veins popped out on his neck.

"If I may have your attention, I brought the figures...."

"Our figures show increased levels of ammonia and PAHs in the water," Moss yelled. "We didn't know why, when all of the clean-up efforts had resulted in toxic levels of all kinds finally dropping. Glad to know who to blame. It must be coming down the river from Washington. And now you're manufacturing trouble here."

"That is not true!" Ms. Sloane's mask dropped, her mouth twisting in anger. "I'll have our lawyers…"

Kiyiya raised his hands for silence. Tariq and Moss froze. And, interestingly, so did Patricia Sloane. His voice, when he spoke, carried strong and true over the breeze and the noise from the river and bridge.

"For you, this is about money," he said. "For us, this is about life. And you threaten the life of everything that lives on this river and around its banks. The fish, the birds, the trees and insects, and the humans and other animals, too. You talk a good talk, but all we hear are lies."

Every camera had turned to catch his words.

Moss felt the urgent pressure inside ebb. The kami of the river had been spoken for. That was all it wanted.

For, somehow, the truth to come out.

Moss knew that the results hadn't yet come back in from the tests their rogue biologists and chemists were doing, but he, Tariq, and Kiyiya knew what they would find. So though they spoke the truth, it wasn't yet confirmed. But Alejandro wouldn't have warned him otherwise.

He hoped they could confirm it before Saturday. They needed the ammunition to turn the public tide.

Reporters scrambled forward to talk with Tariq and Kiyiya. Moss's mouth felt filled with ashes. He didn't want to speak with anyone. He stepped backwards, almost knocking into one of the socialist action crew, who patted his back and steadied him. Moss nodded thanks, and pushed his way out of the scrum.

Finally free of the crush of bodies and shouting, he inhaled the brackish breeze. He needed to talk to Alejandro and find out exactly how much he knew.

When Moss looked at the edge of the small crowd, he saw that his coven brother was gone.

But Patricia Sloane's cold green eyes were on him. He stared right back, hackles raised. She blinked, then turned away.

22

SHAGGY

Shaggy stood on the sunny Hawthorne Street sidewalk, staring at a painted window sign that read "The Inner Eye" in a triangle, with one of those old-fashioned woodcut-looking eyes staring out at her. Behind the glass, crystals gleamed on colorful silks, statues of deities danced and posed, and a book display enticed people to come in and browse.

She wasn't certain how she found herself in front of the esoteric shop, except that it was only a couple of blocks from the circus school and when she and Phoebe wrapped up their conversation, she had felt like taking a walk. Her sneakers had led her directly here, then stopped. She had some vague idea that Moss's coven leader—or high priestess, or whatever you called it—owned the place. She also knew that some strange tugging at her solar plexus called her to go inside.

But she stood on the sidewalk as if her feet had grown roots. Oh, it wasn't that Shaggy was afraid of woo-woo stuff. There was plenty of that on the festival circuit. As a matter of fact, it was hard to escape.

It was that Shaggy was afraid that something inside that shop was going to tell her a thing she might not be ready to hear.

"Damn. Just try, Shaggy. Open the door."

As soon as the words were out of her mouth, she felt the weight of them, as if the cosmos had just spoken a message. Okay. Maybe she was a *little* bit afraid of the woo. She forced herself to turn toward the waiting door, and got her feet moving. One step. Two steps. Three. Hand on the knob. Pushing. The chime of bells and some kind of harp music. The scent of frankincense burning.

Her lips were wet. Licking them, she tasted the salt of tears. Was she crying? When had she started crying? Must be the pregnancy hormones. She never cried like this.

She swiped at her face as an attractive white woman with dark hair piled up in a messy bun walked toward her. She wore a flowing blue tunic top over black pants and low boots, and silver jewelry everywhere. The woman looked to be around forty-something, if Shaggy had to guess. Not far off in age from Bianca, at any rate.

"May I help you?" The woman's voice was so kind, Shaggy felt herself tear up again. Where had all of this emotion come from?

"I... Yes. I mean, I don't know."

"Can I point you toward some books? Or crystals? Or would you like a cup of tea?"

"Do you do readings here?"

The woman smiled at her. "We do. And my next client just cancelled, so I've got a spot open right now. Do you have time?"

Shaggy nodded, not trusting her voice.

"All right then. Follow me and we'll get set up." The woman turned and began threading her way through display cases toward a configuration of bookcases and comfy-looking chairs. "I'm Brenda, by the way," she said, turning her head.

"Shaggy."

The woman stopped. "Shaggy? Moss's friend?"

Moss was talking about her? Shaggy felt her face flush with heat, though she didn't know why she should feel embarrassed. "Yes. Moss's friend."

They'd reached the main counter of the shop, where a younger woman with short, platinum-blond hair and tattoos snaking down one arm was ringing up a customer.

"Tempest, it looks like I've got a reading after all. You good here?"

"I'm good, boss," she said with a grin.

Brenda led Shaggy past the bookshelves and statuary toward a small alcove at the rear of the shop. A floor-length, royal-blue curtain was pulled to one side, revealing a small table and two chairs. As they drew closer, Shaggy could see that the table held a candle, a little brass bell, and a deck of brightly colored cards. Tarot.

Shaggy had gotten readings a time or two at festivals. The last reading she gotten, she'd been high. Other than the flashing colors and the gentle presence of the reader, she recalled nothing. Well. Except for the important part. The one sentence that had pierced through her MDM cloud.

"If you don't choose your destiny, who will?"

The words still echoed in Shaggy's head when she woke up the next morning. Walking toward the reading table now, following the witch, they rose up like a prayer.

"Why don't you have a seat?" Brenda gestured to one of the chairs before pulling out her own. She waited as Shaggy fumbled her purse from her shoulder and slung it over the back of the chair. When Shaggy finally settled, she found herself staring into blue eyes filled with kindness and understanding. With a flick and a tug, Brenda closed the blue curtain around them, shutting out the shop and, it felt like, the world.

Shaggy released a breath she hadn't even realized she was holding in, and felt her body relax. She felt safe here. Protected. And looking at those blue eyes again, she wanted nothing more than to spill her whole life story to this woman.

If only she could figure out where to begin.

"Let's start with something simple, shall we?" Brenda said, as if she'd heard the thoughts that tumbled inside Shaggy's head. She picked up the deck and, bracelets chiming together, began to shuffle. The card edges snapped together and a wash of colors flew between her hands. Again and again, she shuffled, until Shaggy was half mesmerized by motion and sound. Finally, she stopped and placed the deck in front of Shaggy.

"Cut the deck into three piles."

Shaggy reached out, and split the deck into three uneven stacks, setting them next to one another on the table.

Brenda considered the piles for a moment, her fingers hovering just above the cards before resting on the one dead center. She picked that up and stacked it on top of the other two, forming them into one deck again.

"Okay. Let's begin with past, present, and future."

Her graceful fingers snapped three cards out onto the table.

"Ten of Wands. Two of Swords. The World."

The images seared themselves into Shaggy's mind. A figure carrying a heavy burden of sticks, clearly weighted down. A blindfolded person, sitting in front of a body of water, holding two swords crossed over their chest. And last, a figure in the center of a wreath, holding two candles, looking as if they were dancing in the sky.

"What do they mean?"

Brenda tapped the first card with a pale fingernail. "This one, the recent past, shows you carrying far too much. Unnecessary burdens. Other people's problems. Worry. The feeling that you need to do it all, and control it all."

"Well, shit," Shaggy said, then clapped a hand over her mouth.

Brenda just laughed. "Well, shit, indeed. Now, the Two of Swords tells us that you are in stasis regarding a big choice." She trained those blue eyes on Shaggy again. "In Tarot, swords are the mind, and you've been trying to make a decision using your head, which is why you're at an impasse. But see all the water in this card?"

Shaggy nodded.

"In this context that tells us the decision hinges on the emotions, not just your brain. And that brings us—and you —to The World. The dancer in the cosmos. The one who has completed one cycle and is ready to dance into the next. How about it, Shaggy? Are you ready for the next cycle?"

Shaggy nodded again, then shook her head. Then burst into tears.

23

MOSS

Moss felt amped up and furious. It took every ounce of his will to keep his feet and hands still. Arrow and Crescent Coven was gathered in Raquel's living room, every single member present and accounted for.

He sat on a cushion on the floor, spine propped up against the big red couch, and glanced up at the beautiful painting of Raquel's son, Zion, as the Tarot card image of the Sun. Moss wished for the happy, carefree feeling that the card evoked. Shit, he'd felt that just a few days ago, at the club. That night felt like it was two months ago. This year had been a trash fire of disaster after disaster. He supposed he shouldn't call it that, thought forms having power and all. Besides which, that wasn't a hundred percent fair. The coven had had a lot of victories, and so had the larger community.

But it barely felt that way now. Right this minute? Moss wanted to punch something.

"I told you," Alejandro said to Raquel, "I quit, but I still can't really talk about it. You should be looking at Moss about this."

The two witches were faced off, Alejandro in one of the

chairs near the cold fireplace, and Raquel ensconced on one corner of the couch. Moss could feel the ice emanating from Raquel's gaze as she bored two holes into Alejandro's head.

"Have you wondered why you even considered working for a company that puts our communities in danger?" Raquel's voice was flat, the way she got when she was a certain kind of angry. Moss was glad she wasn't mad at him.

It seemed like half the coven was on edge and pissed off. He could also feel Tempest and Tobias using their energy fields to try to smooth things out and keep the energy from spiraling out of control.

"Why don't we all take a breath?" Tempest asked.

"I am not done," Raquel said. "What do you mean I should ask Moss? How in Goddess's name is any of this on him? Alejandro?"

"Raquel…" Brenda started. It seemed she'd finally decided that watching and waiting was no longer enough, and was stepping into the fray.

Raquel held up a hand toward Brenda, which only escalated the tension.

This was getting ridiculous, and wasting time. Moss decided enough was enough. He set his mug on the coffee table and waved his hands in the air.

"Can you all just chill for a minute? This is getting us nowhere, and the action is on Saturday and we need to figure out what the fuck we're going to do. The company is GranCo. I know it now. That's what Alejandro means. We were both out at the fucking press conference today. Before you walked away."

Alejandro just shrugged and took a sip from the green tumbler in his hand. "GranCo is not my client, even if I still can't confirm the name of who was. I refused the contract. So, get off my fucking back."

Brenda gave Moss a slight smile and leaned back in her chair, bracelets chiming and moonstone pendant winking at him from where it rested on her blue tunic top.

"Thank you, Moss, I agree. Alejandro? I'm sure you're making decisions to the best of your ability right now. And we need to trust that, we need to trust each other. But for right now, it seems we're being called upon to do our best to protect the Willamette. Raquel? I know you have a special relationship with her, and I'm wondering if you and Moss could work together to figure out what is needful. And to figure out what this egregore is that Moss is sensing. As a matter of fact, I think we should go upstairs and the two of you should go into trance and figure this out."

The energy in the room shifted, and Moss could practically feel Tempest and Tobias sigh with relief. Even Selene came back from whatever shadowy realm they had retreated to.

Raquel shook out her hands and rolled her neck, as if she could disperse the anger trapped inside her body. Moss exhaled in a huge rush, and then did the same. It wasn't enough. He stood up and shook out his hands and his feet and bounced for a while, trying to shake out all the tension that had been accumulating since he first saw the crack across his windshield.

"Good idea, Moss," Tempest said. She sprang to her feet and began to bob and shake along with him. Slowly, one by one, every member of Arrow and Crescent Coven followed suit.

"Do you have a smudge stick down here, Raquel?" Selene asked.

"There's a rosemary and lavender bundle on the hearth."

Soon the scents of fragrant herbs twined through the air. Selene walked the rough edges of the circle made by the coven members and living room furniture. Their long dark hair formed a loose curtain around their head, and their lips were pale today, almost matching the moonstone at their collarbone. Not quite as large as Brenda's, it was an impressive magical amulet all the same.

Moss breathed in the rosemary and lavender smoke, and closed his eyes, feeling for the still center at his core, the space he'd worked so hard to identify and grow. There it was, half buried beneath his fear, agitation, and anger. He sent a breath down into his belly, imagining the inhalation expanding the small pool of stillness. Moment by moment, breath by fragrant breath, he felt his equilibrium return.

Opening his eyes, he found Raquel looking at him, her dark eyes questioning, her body coiled in waiting. He nodded her way.

"You want to do this?" he asked.

"Much as I'd rather ride my anger into war with these polluting bastards right now? I have to admit that Brenda's right and some psychic reconnaissance is in order. Upstairs?" She jerked her head toward the hallway with a shake of her dreadlocks.

"Why don't we just do it here?" Moss asked. "I don't feel like spending more time setting up."

"Okay. Lucy? Or Tempest? Want to take us down?"

"I'll do it," Tempest replied, stepping forward. "But can we at least get this coffee table out of the way?"

Lucy and Tobias waited while folks cleared cups and books from the table, then hoisted it over the couch and set it in the hallway while Selene lit some candles on the fireplace mantle.

Moss and Raquel each grabbed a cushion and plopped down on the floor, Moss lying down flat, and Raquel sitting cross-legged, with a straight back. The rest of the coven remained standing in a loose circle.

"Slow your breathing down," Tempest began. "Find your center. Relax your edges. Soften your attention and allow your consciousness to float. Become a drop of water, traveling west, seeking to join the river."

"Yemǫja, mother, hear your daughter, reveal to me what needs to be revealed," Raquel said, her voice like honey, her words slow as molasses.

Moss felt his consciousness deepen, and the space between each breath grow vast. He allowed himself to stretch out, and reached for the flow of the great Willamette. He clapped three times. When his mind and heart had contact, he felt the kami of the river respond.

Deep inside his trance state, he smiled. His consciousness dropped another layer down. Deeper. So deep.

Moss was floating in the river, surrounded by cool, murky, blue-green water. Green lichen floated by, followed by a shimmering school of sturgeon. Weak, pale green light filtered in from above. He knew it was the sun. He felt the way the sun on the water interacted, and the way the birds and the fish interacted. He felt the oxygen in the water, and the trees that rooted themselves on the banks on either side. And he was of the river, and from the river, and in the river.

And Moss became the river. The spirit of the river entered him, and spoke in a voice so clear and deep, resounding like the striking of a gong.

::I am the lifeblood of the city, and I am more than that. I give pleasure to the people, and sustenance to the creatures and the plants. And all of these are of me and in me, and I am all of these, but I am also something more. I am the conduit to the ocean. I taste the sky in the fall of rain. And I am choking from these poisons, but I shall. Not. Die.::

Moss's awareness lifted slightly, and he could smell the beeswax of the candles, and feel the coven around his physical body. He was Moss, and he was river. He was the river, and simply a small man. And all of it was true.

He heard Raquel murmuring, "The Goddess of the fertile waters is ready, and the people must rise. She will fill the people with her blessing, and offer them the food of restoration. The waters have been dishonored, and honor must be restored. A spirit poisons the waters, a spirit controlled by human beings. We do not yet know its name, but its presence is felt in the poison. Follow the poison. Find the people. The waters will run clean."

Moss was yanked back down beneath the surface, and the words of the river's spirit tumbled from his lips. "I call my children to me. I call my children to bless themselves with the waters of life. I call upon my children to dance and sing and fight, until the waters once again flow clean. Follow the banks of the river. Dive deeply. Root. Then fly."

"From the great above, to the great below," Raquel's voice joined his, "the people and the rivers are one. The people and the earth are one. There is no separation. All must be rejoined."

"All must re-enter the flow."

Moss's breath shuddered in his chest. He felt the spirit of the river recede, leaving him, a man lying on a living room floor, surrounded by the people he loved.

Slowly, he blinked and sat up, wincing at the ceiling light overhead.

He reached for Raquel's hand and grasped it.

"I'm going to do some shit on Saturday," he said. "Some comrades and I will be chaining up and locking ourselves down to the bridge, and I want you all nearby. We'll need every ounce of your protection and love."

He looked at Raquel then. "But that means I'll need my witches to help with the egregore, whatever it turns out to be. I'm pretty sure it's anchored to Patricia Sloane, though. There's something up with her that I don't like at all. I'm not sure I can lock down and focus on that kind of magic at the same time."

"You know I'm in," Raquel replied, then looked around the circle. "And I'm sure everyone else in this room is, too."

"Are you sure about locking down, Moss?" Alejandro said. "Isn't the egregore...?"

"Locking down, tethered with community, is part of my magic. And there are enough other people here that can..."

Alejandro leaned forward. "Yeah, but you're the one that saw it around Patricia Sloane. No one else has that connection."

Moss's reply stopped inside his mouth, as if the words were stuck there. He closed his eyes, tried to sense what the answer was.

::*Follow the course.*:: the river said.

But what was the *right* course?

"Any one of you can take on an egregore," he finally replied. "But I'm the only one in this room that's able to lock down."

He looked around the circle at the people that had become his second family.

"I'll do my magic. I trust you to do yours."

24

SHAGGY

Shaggy sat in a corner table of one of the Hawthorne Street cafés, still reeling from the reading, and meeting Brenda, and all the rest of it. She barely noticed the other customers coming and going, the small tables filling and emptying, the early '90s music playing over the speakers. The mingled scents of coffee and herbal teas.

The images of the cards still flashed through her mind. The person, bowed and burdened with a bundle of sticks. The woman holding two swords, blindfolded. And the World card...

She needed to stop stalling. Decisions had to be made, and that meant, in order to make an informed choice, she needed to talk with Moss. She also knew he wasn't going to want to talk about what was on her mind. Being an honorable guy, he was going to want to discuss the zygote.

Shaggy sighed and checked the time on her phone. Moss was meeting with the coven now, she knew, but he'd replied to her text, saying he would swing by to meet her as soon as he could get away. So she sipped at her peppermint tea and waited, picking at a cinnamon scone that had been fresh in the morning but now veered toward stale. Shaggy needed the calories, but couldn't manage to eat much.

What she really wanted was a glass of wine, but she'd been drinking too much in the past week, and knew it. Whether she was keeping the zygote or not, she needed to slow down with the alcohol.

Other than hormones, she wasn't sure why she'd burst into tears in front of Brenda. The cards had felt powerful, and it was clear that she was at some sort of nexus point. It wasn't just about the baby, or moving to Portland, or about school and being away from her family for the first time, or any of the rest of that. It wasn't about Moss either, though she still felt conflicted about him. She now realized if it weren't for the pregnancy, she wouldn't feel any conflict at all. And she would just take time and get to know him, the way she imagined other people did. See if they could work something out.

She hadn't felt attracted to someone the way she did Moss for a long time, if ever. Frankly, while she was taking care of her dad, she just hadn't had time for it. Oh, she'd had plenty of sex and short-term relationships, but nothing that she felt like she maybe wanted it to last. She wondered if all that possibility was ruined now.

Ruined by the prospect of a baby.

"It sure makes things more complicated," she muttered under her breath. At any rate, the cards pointed to something big and Shaggy was starting to get an inkling of what that was. For the first time in her life, she wanted something she did to matter. Not her mother's money, not her father's success. Shaggy. On her terms.

She wanted to matter.

The door opened, and in walked Moss, brow creased and mouth drawn with worry. He wore a long sleeved, green

Earth First T-shirt with a fist on it, under that big, gray, knitted cowl he liked. She gave a little wave and he headed to the table, weaving his way through the other two tops before swinging a messenger bag from his shoulder and dropping it into the chair across from hers.

"Do you need anything else?" His smile was swift, half-distracted.

"I'm good, thanks."

"I'll be right back."

Shaggy fidgeted with a napkin as he ordered, wondering how to even start this conversation.

Finally, he was back, setting down a cup of coffee and bag of salt and pepper chips. Strange combination, but whatever made him happy.

"So, I'm glad you texted," he said.

Shaggy felt her face burn.

"Yeah, I'm sorry I put you off, but I've just had a lot to process, you know?"

He was silent, stirring his coffee, waiting for her to finish her thoughts.

Damn. Just when it would've been useful to have a blowhard who wanted to leap in and start asking questions, she had to get a patient man.

"Before I decide whether or not to stay pregnant—but you should know I'm leaning against—there's a couple things I need to talk to you about."

Moss shifted in his chair, as if he was uncomfortable and wanted to leave. Then he inhaled, straightened up, and faced her head on. As if he'd made an internal decision. He looked calmer and less worried, and more present somehow. She wondered if it was some witchy thing.

"The other day, when we were talking, you mentioned a friend of yours. An organizer..."

"Terra?" he asked.

"Yeah." She lowered her voice and leaned forward. "You know I study aerial work, right?"

He nodded.

"Well, I talked with my teacher and we were wondering if you all could use some help with Saturday's action. I remembered you said Terra trains people to do banner drops and stuff, and I'm wondering if she has the equipment to keep us tethered to the bridge."

He leaned back and huffed out a breath. "Damn. That is so not what I expected this conversation to be about. We should power down our phones."

"What?"

"Security," he said, taking his phone out of his pocket. Shaggy did the same.

"All the way off?"

He nodded and watched as she complied. Then he leaned across the table this time. "You really want to suspend yourselves from the bridge? You can actually *do* that?"

Shaggy nodded, excitement brewing in her chest. "If we have the right safety equipment, we can rappel down on colored silk, right over the water."

"That is so freaking cool. Wow. Shaggy?" He looked at her with a cocky grin on his face, not distracted anymore. "You're in. We're going to make this happen."

"Really?" Optimism bloomed inside her chest for the first time in way too long.

Moss nodded and picked up his coffee again. "But after we get through this weekend, I really hope you'll let me in on the pregnancy stuff. I'm not going to be an ass about it, but...I still need something. You know?"

Shaggy snaked a hand across the table and touched the fingers that wrapped around the mug, just briefly.

"I know."

But she was glad to have a few days' reprieve, and something fresh and exciting to focus on. Something that might make a difference in this world.

25
———————

MOSS

oss walked past the closed shops on Hawthorne with a spring in his step, smelling the cool autumn evening. After the conversation with Shaggy, he felt relieved, even a little bit excited. They'd even shared a sweet, chaste kiss before parting ways. After all the anger and frustration from earlier, his heart felt light. He still didn't know what was going to happen between him and Shaggy, but at least now she was talking to him. Baby or not, that alone made it feel like everything was going to be okay.

He turned off the main drag, heading into the darker residential streets. He loved the houses here, the old Craftsman-style bungalows, with an occasional, peak-roofed Victorian dandy thrown in. Clustered in the yards lit by the dim yellow streetlights overhead still grew wild riots of flowers and late vegetables, grown by homeowners who lovingly tended them. Their own small way of trying to change the world. The scent of night blooming jasmine wafted by. Its scent would linger through October.

None of his close friends could afford a house in this neighborhood. Maybe fifteen or twenty years ago, but not anymore. His coven mate Selene's boyfriend lived around here somewhere, but must have bought during a dip in the market, he guessed.

Laughter boomed from across the street, two men on a late night dog walk, with a Siberian husky and a great Dane in competition to see who could tug harder on their leashes. The men fought the dogs valiantly, but it was clear this was a struggle they went through every day. Moss smiled. Maybe someday his life would feel settled enough to get an animal companion, but for now, he had to think ahead to Saturday's action, and the magic the coven was planning, hooking Shaggy up with Terra...and fixing his damn windshield.

As he approached his car, the spiderweb of cracks caught the streetlight, and his heart sank. Right. Shit.

"Nothing to be done about it right now."

Oh, the coven had offered to lend him money, and he knew his parents would front for it, too, if it came to that, but Moss hated asking anyone for that kind of help. He still had a lot of unease around money, and all the systems around it. Raquel told him that constriction was affecting the flow of his magic, and she was probably right.

"Just because we're working to dismantle these systems, doesn't mean we don't live inside of them, Moss. You've got to learn to make some kind of peace with it all, or you'll just keep tripping, and cutting your magic off at the knees."

Despite the mixed metaphors, Moss knew his mentor was right. But that didn't mean he'd figured it out yet. It was probably going to take a shit ton of shadow work, and he always felt like there was too much else on his plate to take that on.

He smacked his palm on the roof of the car before fishing out his keys. With a swift apology to the kami of the car for the blow, he unlocked and opened the door. Flinging his messenger bag in the passenger seat, he got in. Once the car was powered up, he connected his phone. Francis and the Lights began to play. Singing along, he pulled out, heading north, then west. His brakes felt a little funny at the stop sign, but then he felt the regenerative brake system push through to the ordinary friction brakes. He exhaled in relief. Must just be touchy because of the weather change or something. Spring and autumn were always weird for temperature, moisture levels, the whole thing.

Moss continued through the residential neighborhood. The street fed him onto the busy thoroughfare of Cesar Chavez, all streetlights, grocery stores, and bars.

He turned north, continuing up Cesar Chavez, mind filled with Shaggy, their brief kiss, and the upcoming action. The Willamette still tugged at his solar plexus and the night's working with Raquel and the coven hummed in his body, flowing through his bloodstream. He barely noticed that the light had changed until it was almost too late.

"Shit!"

Hitting one of the city's ubiquitous potholes, Moss tapped his brakes, felt them engage, and pushed all the way down. Nothing. Pumped again. Nothing.

Moss gripped the steering wheel, grit his teeth, and pressed his foot down a third time. He down shifted as the car slid toward the busy intersection. In desperation, he yanked at the parking brake. Blinding lights flashed at his left side. His body jerked sideways against the seatbelt. Unearthly grinding sound. Pressure. Pain. The scent of blood. Moss hissed through his teeth.

Then everything went black.

26

SHAGGY

Moss lay on a queen size bed, half buried beneath a green comforter, purple shadows beneath his eyes. Shaggy perched on the one chair in the room. It was set in a nook under the window, next to a big dresser filled with objects that looked like some sort of altar. It felt strangely intimate to be here in his bedroom, and to see Moss this way, just lying there, looking as if his fire had gone out. The whole situation made her want to crawl under the covers and hold him close, which seemed like a strange response, but there it was.

They weren't quite friends or lovers, but in this moment, they felt tied together all the same.

Alejandro had texted from Moss's phone to tell her Moss had spent half the night in the hospital. She'd felt the beginnings of a panic attack when she read the text. Her heart started beating fast and she could barely breathe, finally ducking her head down between her knees and breathing into her cupped hands.

Yeah. And she was avoiding thinking about *that* response. Her old therapist would call bullshit, but there that was, too. If she could just get through the week, she'd be fine. She always was.

She inhaled, catching the scent of old incense, and stifled a sigh. Moss wasn't hurt badly. He was going to be okay. Just some bruised ribs. Mild concussion.

"So, Alejandro said your brakes failed?"

"They were cut," Moss said, then coughed and reached for the steel water bottle on his bedside table.

Shaggy leaned forward and raked her hands through the short waves of her hair. "Who would want to cut your brakes? What the hell?"

Moss coughed again and winced. His head must be killing him, but other than a small cut on his forehead and the fact that he seemed weak, it hardly looked like he'd been in an accident at all. But that didn't make the whole situation less scary. Shaggy was used to the slow moving, controlled crashes of lingering addiction and disease, not this fast moving shift with the power to alter the course of someone's life.

"Turns out someone's been sending notes to a few of the tribal elders and local activists. Threats. I just found out that Terra got one, too. Kiyiya called after he heard about my accident to tell her about the other notes. How did these people even find out? I mean, there was the big meeting, but we didn't even have a clear target then. GranCo hadn't even had that damn press conference yet."

Shaggy couldn't even begin to fathom the ins and outs of corporate and environmental politics. If she was going to involve herself, she'd have to learn. Right now? She felt completely at sea.

Moss adjusted himself on the pillows and winced again. "Damn that hurts. Everything hurts."

She watched for a moment as he struggled with the cap

of an aspirin bottle before taking it from him, gently. The fact that he barely resisted was a sign of just how weak he was. She lined the arrows up, snapped off the top and dropped two pills into his outstretched hand.

"They didn't give you something stronger?"

"Didn't want it. It's not that bad." He popped the pills into his mouth and downed them with another swig of water. Sighing, he leaned back against his pillows and closed his eyes.

"It doesn't matter how careful we are," he said, "there's always going to be plants at the meetings. That's why we don't discuss any sensitive information, but they know we have plans for Saturday, and the groups involved. I guess it doesn't take much to start a harassment campaign.

"Harassment? You could've been killed!"

He didn't even open his eyes at that, just sighed again, sinking deeper into the pillows. "I made myself a target at that press conference. So they escalated."

Shaggy felt like running or punching something, but forced herself to sit still, breathing in the old incense and the slightly sour smell rising from Moss. She pulled at a hangnail on her thumb until a bead of blood rose up. She wiped it on her jeans.

"You're sure it's this GranCo?" she asked.

"It's probably some people working for them. Hired flunkies. At least that's what we suspect, but the only person who could possibly confirm with some inside knowledge signed an NDA." Moss opened his eyes, and stared at the ceiling, mouth set in a hard line.

"Alejandro?"

Moss didn't reply. She took it as a yes.

"That seems...surprising. I mean, it's not like I know any of you very well, but I would think he'd be on your side."

"He is," he finally said, struggling to sit up again. "And he refused the contract. That doesn't make the NDA less frustrating, though."

"Are you all going to cancel the action?"

"Because of some threats?"

"Because your brakes were cut!"

"Hell no. The action is happening. These assholes don't control us. Besides, the equinox celebration is an ongoing tradition. Some white corporate shills aren't going to disrupt that."

"But all the stuff you had planned, the lockdown?"

Moss looked her dead in the eye then, his face fierce. "We're going forward. *I'm* going forward."

Well damn. Shaggy admired his determination, but also couldn't imagine going through what sounded like an ordeal so soon after a car crash.

"You sure that's a good idea?"

"Look, Shaggy, you and the coven and everyone else mean well, I know that, but if I'm well enough to stand on Saturday? I'm well enough to lock down for the river."

"That sounds pretty stupid."

"Yeah, well..."

They stared at each other for a while, not speaking. Shaggy finally broke the staring contest, and let her eyes roam around his room. She liked it, she realized, having barely taken in anything other than the altar and the bed the whole time she'd been here. Her focus had been on him. On Moss. Somehow, the room made her like him more, too. The artwork on the walls, the altar, the feeling of sun on the back of her neck through the sheer curtains...it all felt homey. Comforting. Two things she hadn't felt for a long time, not even in her expensive condo filled with furniture she'd picked out herself.

Finally, she turned back to him and nodded. Her heart was beating fast, but she couldn't let fear stop her. She didn't want to.

"All right then. If you're in, I'm still in. What else do I need to do to prepare?"

"You meditate?"

"A little."

"Well, buckle down. You're going to need to be as centered as you can to deal with any possibility that might get thrown at us. Screaming crowds. Cops. The wind whipping you around under the bridge. Whatever. You have to be strong enough to face it all."

His brown eyes still held that fierce light, and Shaggy realized that he seemed a little less sick than when she'd first arrived. His body might be weak, but was stronger than she could have possibly suspected.

Fuck, she thought. He's not just some EDM raver dude. He's actually a man. *An adult. A person I could really fall in love with.*

"Shaggy?" His eyes were questioning.

She licked her lips and rubbed her hands over her jeans.

"Yeah. I can do that. If you can face it, so can I."

Shaggy still wasn't sure exactly what her destiny was, but it seemed that this part of it, at least, was tied up with his.

Eyes still locked on his, slowly, oh so slowly, she leaned over him, giving him the chance to turn his head or move away. He barely even blinked.

Their lips touched. Slightly, gently.

It felt sweet.

27

—————

MOSS

Behind its rusted metal and glass façade, the cavernous warehouse in northeast Portland spent most of its current incarnation as an alternative arts and performance space.

Moss's body was killing him. The cold concrete floor made his already aching joints and bruised ribs want nothing more than to crawl back home and into a warm bath. Shit. He had no clue how dancers managed to rehearse in this space. How in the world did they ever limber up?

"Hey Moss, good to see you!"

He turned at the warm voice. Julia. She was one of the older cis women who'd been a Portland activist fixture for decades. Soft spoken and ever present, Julia did everything from sweeping floors to organizing marches and blockades. Some of the young hotheads thought she wasn't worth listening to, which pissed Moss off.

"Julia, thanks! Good to see you, too."

Her gray and brown hair was styled in its usual messy

brush cut and her battered Doc Martens had been fixed with silver duct tape. She smelled like lemon candy.

"Hug?" she asked, holding out her arms.

"Gotta be careful, I'm pretty banged up, but yeah."

Julia enfolded carefully him into warm, soft arms. As he pressed into her broad chest, Moss sighed. Safe. He held back the tears that threatened to fill his eyes.

As Julia stroked his hair, all the pain, fear, and anger Moss had been clinging to relaxed and slowly floated away. They breathed together for what was likely only seconds, but felt much longer.

The sounds of the meeting starting filtered into his ears, and he tensed, hissing as muscles contracted around his ribs.

"Shh. They can start without us. Just rest for another minute."

He let himself relax again.

"You've been working yourself too hard. As a matter of fact, you know you shouldn't even be here, right?"

Moss laughed and pushed himself away from her embrace. Swiping moisture from his face, he sighed again.

"Thanks, Julia. Yeah. A bunch of people told me to stay home, but I had to be here. Too much at stake."

He looked at her watery brown eyes. She was so damn kind.

"And frankly," he said, "I'm too angry to just lie around."

"All right. Go get 'em. But you let me know if you need anything. And I mean that."

"Thanks, Julia. You're the best." He gave her arms a squeeze and scanned the room for Tariq. His comrade stood closer to the front, in a group off to one side of the chairs.

Squirrel, one of the younger anarchists, paced in the

center of the large group that stood or sat in white folding chairs or directly on the hard concrete floor. Wearing a red bandana around his pale white neck, black skinny jeans, black sneakers, and a black and white T-shirt, he was thin and always animated. Moss didn't know if the guy was powered by sugar, like a hummingbird, or just naturally wired.

"Hey man, I saved you a chair." Tariq gestured to a folding chair at his side. Moss almost groaned, knees and rib cage twinging as he eased his way down.

"Thanks, man. You have no idea," Moss murmured.

"They've attacked our comrades," Squirrel said, "and this will not stand! The Black Rose has license plates from at least two of the reported incidents of rocks being thrown at cars and in two cases, at people on bicycles. We're ready to dox these fuckers!"

Doxxing was serious business, and only done when there was a direct threat to people's safety. Moss didn't have strong opinions on it one way or another. It was just another tactic, and as long as people weren't using it to hurt people who weren't an actual threat? Well... He shrugged inside.

Squirrel's head whipped around, green eyes landing on Moss. Moss's throat and mouth were dry. He'd left his water bottle at home. Wished he'd asked Julia for a lemon drop.

Squirrel swept an arm toward Moss. "They put our comrade here into the hospital. They slaughtered Heather Heyer in Charlottesville, killed three people on the MAX train, and have beaten and sexually assaulted we don't know how many others. What are we gonna do about this?"

Moss waved an arm, then hissed in pain.

"Wait a minute," he croaked out. "Tariq, man, you got water?"

Squirrel paused in his frenetic pacing and waited, foot

tapping, while Tariq took the lid off his steel water bottle and passed it to Moss.

The water felt glorious going down Moss's throat. *All water is one water*, he thought, then cleared this throat and spoke.

"As a Japanese American, I'm down with facing white supremacy and kicking it in the teeth"—he cleared his throat—"but these aren't the same people. Let's not get mixed up about that. This is some bad corporate magic, man. These are people out to destroy the river. We need to act accordingly. The threat to all these activists and elders is a threat to the whole city, just like the racists and fascists are. But let's be strategic here, and not go off with only half the information."

Some activists were always willing to join the fray, which was great, but damn, they lacked strategy. And there was always a protest where every damn group under the sun showed up to push its cause, instead of rallying around the focus of the march or gathering.

Tariq placed a supportive hand on Moss's shoulder before speaking.

"This is *institutionalized* racism and *corporate* fascism that affects St. John's and the rest of Portland," Tariq said, "not an organized group of racist hotheads. With the elders' permission, we'll be facing the threat head on this Saturday, and want all bodies who can be, in Cathedral City Park. And if Black Rose has damning information on these attacks? All the better. We can use it as ammunition, try to trace it back to these corporate vampires. Thanks as always, comrades."

"We need to remember that the folks who live in North Portland have been under attack for decades," Moss chimed in. "The poisoning of the river...after the Yakama, Chinook, and other indigenous leaders, the Black Environmental

Group, and the Clean Rivers Coalition put in years of labor holding groups accountable and getting the water as clean as they could? This is not only a slap in the face, it's a danger to all our communities, as much of a danger as the white supremacists we've all worked so hard to get out of our city. The rivers need us, and we need the rivers."

Moss grabbed Tariq's hand and got help to stand up. Goddesses, his body hurt!

He slowly turned to address the people gathered in the cavernous space.

"You with us on this?"

The people lifted their fists and shouted "Yes!"

28
———

SHAGGY

haggy and Phoebe walked through the little neighborhood of Cathedral Park, past bungalows and single story Victorian houses. The sun was out for the third day in a row, though rain was forecast for the following week. It was a sweet place, filled with trees and bordering the Willamette in North Portland, a neighborhood Shaggy had never visited before. Terra had agreed to meet them at the park itself beneath the St. John's Bridge. As they approached the towering green gothic structure set on massive concrete arches, she saw a powerful-looking Black woman around her own age. She talked on a cell phone, one foot resting on a park bench, eyes trained down the sloping green dotted with birches and what might be cherries, past a huge maple tree, leaves turning orangey gold, to where the the river flowed.

Terra must've sensed their approach, because she quickly ended her phone call, shoved her phone into the pocket of her cargo pants and gave a slight wave, heading across the grass toward the cement walkway that ran beneath the bridge and up to a set of stairs leading a small parking lot.

Shaggy strode forward, trying to act more confident than she actually felt in the moment. She could feel sweat under her arms, despite the mild day, and hoped Terra couldn't see how nervous she actually was. As they got to within a foot or two Shaggy stuck out a hand.

"Terra? I'm Shaggy and this is Phoebe."

Terra enfolded one of Shaggy's hands in her own. Her skin was warm, and she smelled like peppermint gum.

"Thanks for meeting with us," Shaggy said.

"No problem," Terra replied. "Moss wouldn't have hooked us up if you weren't cool." Terra gave a slight smile at that, which lit up her whole face. "Both your phones off?" Shaggy and Phoebe nodded. They'd taken care of that in the car. Moss's basic training was starting to kick in.

"Good. Let's walk." Terra led them back out from underneath the bridge. Then they were on an open green past some birches and the maybe-cherries, at the edge of several tall, raggedy edged firs. No one was around except one dog walker and a lone kayak paddling in a small, protected lagoon. Terra stopped and turned. "So, you actually want to rappel down from the bridge? Do either of you have experience with that?"

Keeping her hands low, she gestured up at the green steel expanse.

Shaggy squinted at Terra, half-dazzled by the sun and half-hoping Phoebe would answer.

"I have a lot of experience working with safety harnesses in different situations," Phoebe replied, "and Shaggy has gotten pretty good at aerial work. I'm willing to train her on the rest."

"By tomorrow? That seems pretty risky."

"We know that," Shaggy said, "but if I can do aerial work without a harness twenty feet in the air, I'm pretty sure I can do it *in* a harness, no problem."

"No problem!" Terra laughed at that. It was clear she was skeptical but that didn't matter. All that mattered was that she would get them the equipment, even if the thought half-terrified Shaggy.

Shaggy and Phoebe both paused, staring at Terra, listening to the seagulls squawking nearby. All three women just stared at each other for a moment, no one willing to cede ground. Finally, Terra shrugged.

"All right. Plan is to rappel down from the central section of railing there, past that big support, where the bridge heads over the river. Right? You want to be over the water itself, and not the park here?"

"Right," Phoebe replied.

"Okay. I'll be anchoring one of you, and have a second person on board. We'll also be taking care of a banner drop. Usually we'd work on this for weeks, but I'm going to trust you, and you're just going to have to trust me and my team. I've got two harnesses and the rest of the gear in the car. I'm parked just over there. You got a car?"

"A few blocks away," Phoebe replied.

"Meet me in the lot, then. But Phoebe? Anything goes wrong with this tomorrow and it's on you. My team will do our best, but you're new to us...and frankly, we argued about whether or not to even help you do this. Also, we're going to have our hands full with a lot of other stuff. Okay?"

"Okay."

"And Shaggy? Stay safe, will you? Moss will kill me if something bad happens to you."

Shaggy gave the other woman a tight smile and a nod. "Got it."

Phoebe loped off toward the car, Shaggy trailing behind her. They had all afternoon to practice at the circus school. Phoebe had already cleared a corner of the room on the school schedule. They could practice into the night if they had to. Shaggy really hoped it would be enough.

Butterflies filled her belly, and she didn't know which sense was stronger: excitement, or fear.

All she knew was, despite the danger, it still felt right.

29

MOSS

Moss and most of Arrow and Crescent, along with a few of their close allies, were gathered on Brenda's forest-green couches and creamy linen-covered footstools, making plans for the next day. Her living room was soothing. It had pale green walls, and bright artwork of a variety of Goddesses and Gods. Over the fireplace mantle was a brilliant painting of the sun dancing with the moon.

Raquel's buff, Thor-looking boyfriend Charlie give her thigh a squeeze. Watching that made Moss wish Shaggy was there, but her text said she and Phoebe were busy practicing with the safety gear "for a big show coming up." That made him smile. In one short week, he'd been cramming as much security culture training into her as possible. Encrypted text system or not, nothing was foolproof. Oblique messages were best.

He needed to meet with the lock-down crew later himself. A few of them were doing reconnaissance at the bridge, figuring out the best places to lock down to block the span.

Shaggy had said he could swing by her place after he

was done with it all. He wanted to. More than anything. He also needed to keep his head in the game. If he swung by, they would have sex. He could feel it. And he wanted it. That meant that despite his messed-up body, a late night, and an even earlier morning, he was probably going to comply with the urge to see her. To touch her. To reassure himself that life was worth living and that the battle to come would not, could not, be the end.

He rolled his shoulders, trying to release the tension, and was just reaching for some gluten-free cookies when Brenda's door opened again and Alejandro walked in.

At first glance, he was neat as a pin, but looking more closely, Moss saw Alejandro's lavender shirt wasn't as well pressed as usual, and one of the lenses on his glasses had a streak down the side.

"Should you be here, hermano?" Lucy said.

Alejandro threw up his hands. "They can't prove I told you anything, especially since I haven't."

"Is that actually true?" Jack asked. Jack was Lucy's new boyfriend and a coder and had been a friend of the coven for years. "They could still claim we got information from you, even if we found it out ourselves. That could bite you in the ass, badly."

"Us, too," Selene remarked from their perch on a velvet tuffet that looked designed especially for the femme Goth that they were. "Especially Moss."

Alejandro shrugged, looked around the room, and dragged a cushion next to Selene before sinking down. "Frankly, let them. I'm so furious at what they're doing, what their plans are, and that damn press conference stunt they pulled, that I..." He ran his hands across his hair—a sign of distress, Moss realized—before looking up again. "I'm done. I'm done with *all* of these pendejos, and that includes half of my current client list. There's too much gray area in my life. What am I going to tell my nieces and nephews that I do, huh? That I make money from corporations that green wash and pink wash their sins? I've got to figure something else out."

Raquel reached over and ran a hand down his arm. "Hey. We got you. We've always got you. You'll figure it out. Besides, you already have more money than anyone else in this coven,"

"Put together!" Lucy interrupted.

"Put together," Raquel said. "In other words, you're smart, you've got a great portfolio, and you. Have. Time."

"I'm glad you're here, man," Moss said to his friend. And he was. It had felt really weird to even briefly be on opposite sides of something with a man he had been able to trust with his life. "And we live under capitalism. No money is clean."

"Yeah, well..." Alejandro waved a hand, making Moss smile. Alejandro would never say he wasn't a capitalist, and Moss loved to point out all the ways the system rubbed his coven brother wrong.

Brenda poured some sparkling water into a clear wine glass and handed it to Alejandro. "We're all glad you're here. And I'm really glad you're making this change. Raquel and I have been a little worried about you. Come by the shop for a reading next week. We'll see what the Gods are cooking."

Alejandro wiped at his eyes, then took his tortoiseshell glasses off and wiped the lenses with the white handker-chief. Only man Moss knew who pressed his hankies.

"Thanks, everyone. Where are we at for tomorrow? And how can I help?"

"We were just figuring that out," Raquel said, leaning forward to grab a piece of cheddar from the wood block on the coffee table. "You'll need magical backup to deal with this egregore, right? Have you figured out any more about it? What can you tell us?"

Moss shook his head. "I'll be in lockdown. Someone else is going to have to deal with it. I thought you would, given your connection to the river."

"You were just in an accident!" The words burst from Raquel's mouth. "And what if the whole river decides to channel itself through your body, locked down or not? It's too dangerous, Moss!"

"It's not going to happen." But he couldn't deny the pressure on his skin. The river. It had been there all week, only growing more intense over the past few days. But he also didn't believe the river kami would take him over that way. No other animating spirit had ever done that before.

"That's not how my magic works. My relationship with the kami is different than your relationship with your matron Goddess."

"And you're sure of that because…?"

"It's never happened before."

Raquel scowled and gave a *hmph*, while Brenda burst into laughter. "Oh, you sweet summer child! How long have you been training with us? You still think something won't happen just because it hasn't before?"

"You think Tonantzin ever took me over like that before I was up there on the roof with all those DHS cops down on the ground, shooting less than lethals?" Lucy bristled. "Come on, man, don't be a douche. Listen to your elders."

Moss chewed his lower lip. "I promised my crew I'd lock down, from the minute we started talking about this action. I don't feel right backing out of it."

"Can your body even handle it?" Alejandro's voice was soft, but insistent.

"Locking down is no different than standing around in the park. What, am I supposed to stay home in bed?"

"Locking down for Goddess knows how many hours," Raquel leapt in, "and getting sawed apart by the fire department, and then dragged away by the Portland cops? Maybe gassed? Cuffed? Having your arms half ripped from their sockets? Come on, Moss. Don't act like we haven't been there with you before." She threw her hands in the air and sat back on Brenda's couch in a huff.

Moss closed his eyes and fought to slow his breathing back down. He felt every twinge in his body, from all the screaming tendons surrounding his left knee to the ever-present headache. He could also feel the pull of the river and the pushing of the kami to *do this thing*.

"Those bastards *threatened* me. They cut my fucking brake lines. I have to lock down. And it isn't just that, or my crew. It's the kami of the Willamette." He held up one hand to forestall objections. "It's not just my ego saying that, either. I can't tell you why, but locking down at St. John's Bridge is the most necessary thing I've done in my life. I'm sure of it. If you want to help me, help me do that. And if some of you want to do your psychic thing and pump me some energetic support or information, that'd be great. But I'm doing this. I have to."

The energy roiling around the room rose, then left in a whoosh, as though a mighty force had opened up the front and back doors and sent a cross breeze wafting through to clear the air.

"Okay," Raquel said. "Nothing else we can do then. We'll honor that, Moss"—she fixed him with her intense, dark eyes—"but don't make me regret this, or I'll kick your damn ass. Now, tell us about the egregore. What do you know?"

Moss exhaled. "Okay. I still don't have a lot of information, so whoever decides to do the astral work will be mostly flying blind. Sorry about that. But I can tell you it seems to be deeply connected to a woman named Patricia Sloane."

Alejandro nodded. "Having seen her, I think you're right. There's something around her that felt off when I shook her hand the other day, but I couldn't place it. Didn't think too much about it, frankly. I was just looking for ways to avoid being roped into that contract."

"So, Raquel, do you think you can deal with this? Or do you want someone else?" Moss asked.

Raquel looked at Brenda, who lifted her hands, silver bracelets chiming.

"You're currently the most qualified," Brenda said. "Between your skill level and the water connection."

"Okay. I'll do it. But I don't like it, Moss, I can tell you that right now. I want Alejandro to back you up, since he has a taste of the egregore. I don't think the river or whatever this entity is, is going to leave you alone, locked down or not. I really don't think it's safe, and if you weren't already an initiate, I'd tell you no." Raquel's dark eyes held his in challenge.

"Fine with me," Moss replied. "We don't have time to argue about it, do we?"

"Your funeral," she said, then looked away.

Great. He just loved pissing off his mentors. Moss sighed.

"Now, who's backing up Raquel, and who's doing whatever else needs doing? I know the tribal elders and the Clean River Coalition could use another couple trusted go-between folks on comms, and the Brown Berets and Sons of Sàngó could likely use security help."

"Any other magic workers gonna be on site?" Lucy asked. "Or is there other magic you two think we should be working on in particular?" She gestured to Raquel and Moss.

"Well, making sure Raquel has what she needs to deal with the egregore is priority. After that, anything that supports the Willamette and reveals the truth about these bastards," Moss said. "That's the magic everyone there is going to be doing, whether they think it's magic or not. So, support the magic every single affinity group is doing. Let the magic do its work."

"Sounds good," Lucy replied. "I'm in."

"Okay," Brenda interjected, "let's figure out who is taking on what role. I don't want to leave any part of this operation to chance."

Moss heard the river whispering inside him. He felt the love he had for every single person in the room.

"Thanks everyone. I couldn't do this without you. And the Willamette couldn't either."

"It takes a village," Alejandro replied. "And this village isn't taking any shit."

Moss smiled.

30

SHAGGY

It was ten o'clock equinox morning, the sun was out, and Cathedral City Park was a gorgeous green expanse beneath the gothic towers of St. John's Bridge. Sun shone on the warm gold leaves of the maple that presided over a copse above a small stage where two people set up a makeshift sound system. Shaggy bet the park was an amazing place in spring. Even on the tail end of summer, the place was breathtaking.

The beauty couldn't distract Shaggy from the fact that fifty-two degrees Fahrenheit with a wind from the east bumping up against the breeze rising off the river itself meant that Shaggy was damn cold. And, frankly, terrified. She looked up at the arched concrete towers that supported the steel suspension bridge on land, and wondered what the hell she thought she was doing. Last night during practice, despite exhausting herself, everything had felt so right. She was excited, and felt sure about it all. The harnesses were a bit of a pain to work with, and it took some doing to not get them tangled in the silks, but she and Phoebe had drilled until her arms and legs shook with effort and sweat soaked through her practice clothes.

And then she'd spent the night in Moss's arms. He'd stumbled in just after midnight, half exhausted, and they'd had a few hours together before he stumbled off again at six, not even staying for the coffee she'd promised him.

The sex had been sweet. Gentle. They had to be careful because of Moss's injuries. The fact that they couldn't just jump each other made things harder for Shaggy this morning. Hot sex she could do in a minute. Sweet sex? That was a lot more difficult. It ended up *meaning* something. And she wasn't ready to face that. Sex that was both sweet *and* hot? No matter how much she wanted it, it made her want to run away.

"You're pretty messed up, Shaggy." She tried to stretch her cold muscles. Phoebe jogged in place a couple of yards away.

"You say something?"

"No. Just talking to myself."

Shaggy bent toward the damp grass on a deep exhalation and touched her forehead to her shins. Her hamstrings screamed, angry at the cold and at the extra-long workout they'd gotten the night before. She eased off immediately. No need to risk injury.

Just like with the sweet sex, she needed to take the stretching slow. If only she could be slow with her heart. It felt sore today, too. Filled with a sadness she barely wanted to acknowledge. A sadness that maybe, just maybe, if she let herself, she could have real love. That was what the cards were telling her, she realized. It had very little to do with the abortion, or her family, or anything else. It was about her tendency to cut and run the minute anyone who mattered wanted in.

And Moss mattered. She couldn't begin to understand why he still insisted on locking down and risking a brutal arrest...but she also knew as a non-activist, and as someone who barely even knew him, there wasn't really anything she could say.

But that didn't mean she didn't worry.

She inhaled the morning air and went back to her stretching, arms pebbled with goosebumps even beneath the long-sleeved leotard and dagged-edged blue fleece festival jacket she had been sure were warm when she'd dressed earlier. Could be worse. She could've been in performance leotards. Phoebe had suggested blue and green to match the river and their blue silks was the way to go, costume-wise, but had wisely suggested they wear something warmer than usual.

Shaggy had unearthed blue velvet festival pants for herself and green ones for Phoebe. Despite leggings beneath the velvet, and her attempts to warm up her muscles, the cold was only going to get worse when the wind high up on the bridge hit. And she hadn't even taken off her shoes and socks yet.

Could she manage the silks in shoes? They were thin-soled sneakers, so maybe?

She looked up again, eyes caught by movement high up in the towers. That would be two of Terra's cohort securing the safety equipment and silks. Both were tied up in small bundles barely visible from the ground. They wouldn't unfurl until Shaggy and Phoebe and the folks doing the banner drop were ready.

Meanwhile, the park was filling up. Some First Nations groups in long skirts and shawls, or decorated jackets and cloth headbands, clustered at one end. There were bunches of people clad all in black, and a variety of folks showing up with banners and signs. She smiled at the group with painted cardboard fish and birds on long poles.

"Look, Phoebe!"

"Those are beautiful!" Her mentor walked closer. "You doing okay?"

"I can't get warm enough, and now that we're here, I'm starting to feel a little scared."

"That's natural," Phoebe replied. "Let's go for a quick jog while we can. It'll warm us up faster than anything else, and take your mind off things. Then we should get ready to head up."

Shaggy swallowed, stomach suddenly sour.

"I don't know if I can do this. I feel sick."

Phoebe assessed her, then shook her head. "Trust me. It's just nerves. Let's jog." She smiled. "You can stop and puke anytime you want to."

"Great. Just great." Shaggy shook her arms out and rolled her head on her shoulders. Phoebe was already jogging away toward the steep flight of concrete stairs beneath the bridge, glancing behind herself to see if Shaggy was coming.

"You said you wanted to do this, Shaggy, so you better get going."

Shaggy took in another breath, and set her sneakers on the path Phoebe had set, increasing her pace until she was jogging right beside her.

"There's no way to tell what's going to happen," Phoebe said between footfalls, "same as with any other performance. So you may as well let it go."

Easier said than done.

31

MOSS

The timing needed to be perfect. If one thing went wrong, the whole lockdown could be botched from the beginning.

At least the day's action didn't rely on the lockdown in order to be effective. Thank all the Gods and kami for multi-pronged community actions.

Moss took in his neighborhood from the front porch of Justice House. He stretched, wincing as various parts of his body pulled and resisted—his ribs still really hurt, and ibuprofen had barely made a dent in the pain—and inhaled the scent of mint and rosemary that grew in pots on either end of the slightly scruffy porch. The day was sunny, but still cool, and he wore boots, baggy jeans, a long-sleeved tee, polar fleece, and his lucky knit cowl.

Moss and his crew had met up at his place at seven in the morning for a quick vegan breakfast supplied by Maggie, bless her, even if she was pissed off at him for locking down. Add another person to his current fan club. She'd even done cleanup so Moss, Barbara Jean, and the others could start loading gear into Tariq's truck and two beat-up old hatchbacks.

Right now, folks carried supplies from other vehicles and from inside Justice House. Their support and propaganda teams would meet them at the bridge, parking offsite and walking on. The lockdown crew would carpool with the gear, taking what they could and consolidating the rest into the three vehicles that would remain on the bridge, forming the first barrier to shut the four lanes down.

The motley crew were cheerful enough, and efficient, working quickly in the cool, late morning air. Everyone had done this before, which was the only reason the group had agreed to a last-minute action. Successful blockades could take weeks—sometimes even months—of careful planning. The more experienced and trusted the people, the less time they needed. Even the support crew that would bring water or snacks, or hold up aching arms, had all done at least one other blockade.

If they were going to block the span, all twenty-five of the people locking down needed to be prepared, mentally and physically, and the chains and PVC tubes were part of that. They'd spent part of last night drilling holes into the center of each four foot length of tubing, and securing bolts into the holes with lug nuts and Gorilla glue. Other people had cut chain, attaching carabiners to the ends so the blockaders could clip themselves to the bolt, once inside the tube.

Moss wore thick socks with the feet cut off over his long-sleeved tee. If you planned to lock down for even a few hours, you needed to be as comfortable as possible. The socks would protect his wrists.

"Got your diaper on?" Tariq asked.

Moss grimaced. "No. I always wait until the last minute. I

hate wearing those." He'd put his loosest jeans on over his boots, though.

"Better than needing to piss or worse, and not having one."

"Yeah, yeah."

There was no denying the physical realities of long blockades, but frankly, wearing adult diapers was still the hardest thing about locking down for Moss. *And how are you going to feel if you're an old man and end up with no choice but to wear them?* He knew his discomfort was just ableist bullshit, but somehow that knowledge didn't make him appreciate the diapers any more.

Moss picked up a load of thick PVC tubes loosely stacked outside the front door, headed down the porch steps, and chucked them into the back of Tariq's old Toyota truck where they clattered with their cousins. He grimaced. Damn ribs. The tubes read *Save the Willamette*, *Greed Pollutes*, and *Water is Life* in thick black Sharpie letters.

Kayakers and at least two sailboats were scheduled to be in the water flying banners with similar messages, and when Shaggy and Phoebe dropped over the water, banners would drop alongside them.

At least that was the plan. First, people would gather in the park, then the tribal elders would do an opening ceremony at the water, followed by a children's choir from St. John's School, then drummers and dancers, back up at the stage. Then, the lockdown. Then, the kayaks, aerialists, and the banner drops. Moss checked his watch. 10:15. That meant the first part of the programming should have started already, or be starting soon. It also meant that rush hour traffic should have died down, which they needed. Tariq would call Terra to check on that before they left for the short drive to the bridge.

The two hatchbacks would wait until Tariq crossed the bridge and doubled back, then they would begin their crossing, stopping as close to mid-span as they could to stop those lanes, while people jumped from the other cars and started setting up the blockade. Tariq would hopefully be able to park his truck across two lanes, blocking traffic on both sides. Their fourth driver had the flu and needed to back out. Tariq would just have to do his best.

Yeah. Damn tricky. All the key people had walkie-talkies to make sure the action went as smoothly as possible. Reconnaissance had found two different spots where they would U-lock the chains on either side. Two spots meant a backup, in case they needed it.

If Terra's crew hadn't been on point to coordinate the rest of the action with the Yakama and Chinook elders, the folks from AIM, and spokespeople from the rest of the affinity groups, Moss would've been a lot more nervous than he was. He had the usual pre-action jitters as the adrenaline built inside his system. As battered as his body felt, he needed the support the rush gave him.

"You okay?" Tariq asked.

Moss jerked at his friend's voice. Friend, comrade, and at one brief point, lovers, until they decided that was too messy with everything else they had going on.

He pushed back from the truck bed. "Yeah. Just worried about Shaggy. She's never done anything like this before."

"Everyone has a first time, right? And Terra won't let them go up if anything looks the slightest bit wrong. You know that, right?"

"Right. Thanks."

Tariq flashed him a lopsided smile and rewound the red bandana that kept his short, tightly coiled locks in place.

"Okay," Tariq said, once he was done, "let's get the rest of this shit loaded. Then, hate to tell you, but you gotta go put your diaper on, man."

"Yeah, yeah," Moss said. "Let's get this done."

One more load of gear, then he'd hit the bathroom. And put that damn diaper on.

His one regret was that he wouldn't be able to see Shaggy in action. He bet it was going to be beautiful.

32

SHAGGY

After Phoebe's enforced running warm-up, Shaggy had to admit her body felt better. Looser. And she was finally warming up.

They walked back down the stairs toward the central circle of concrete under the massive arched supports toward seven dancers in ribbon skirts and bright shawls, and drummers from a local tribe Shaggy didn't know. She would need to learn, she supposed, and should have probably asked before today, but there had been so much going on in the past week she hadn't even thought of it.

The dancers and drummers began a procession leading from the circle and down the small hill toward the river.

She and Phoebe stayed at the rear, not wanting to get caught in the midst of what looked to be a crowd of about two, maybe three hundred, which was quite a lot for such a small park. The people moved toward the greensward that bordered a small estuary and a dock leading to the river itself. Shaggy stopped walking when Phoebe did. They stood on a rise, looking down over the crowd.

Facing the water, an elder native man in a leather vest

with an American Indian Movement back patch raised his hands, rang a bell, and said a prayer in words that flowed like silk. They felt like a scaffolding of fabric Shaggy could climb and dance upon. A second, younger man dipped a clay mug into the water each time, handing it to the elder, who prayed, then passed the mug back to be dipped into the river once again.

Seven times, the bell rang, and seven times, the old man sang and prayed.

Three women in shawls stepped forward. The one with a hoop drum and beater stick started a slow rhythm. Their voices rang out, high and loud, each taking a turn to lead. Everyone gathered faced the water. Not one person raised a camera. Not one person spoke. The only other sounds were the river lapping at the shore, the mallards bobbing in the water, and the distant whoosh of traffic.

The women finished with their prayers and made an announcement that dancing and singing would be happening soon up on the small stage Shaggy had noticed on their way down.

Out on the dock, children dropped flower petals on the river's surface and into the estuary, where they formed vibrant patterns of yellow, pink, blue, and red. It was so beautiful, Shaggy felt tears forming. Maybe Portland was going to turn out to be more than just an escape from Bianca and the past.

Maybe she could belong in a place like this someday.

"We should get going," Phoebe said at her shoulder. "It's almost time to get into our gear."

Shaggy nodded, hands suddenly damp and throat dry. At least the breeze from the east had finally died down, warming up the morning. Maybe she wouldn't need to wear her fleece, and she and Phoebe wouldn't have to battle extra wind beneath the bridge. There were enough other variables to keep track of as it was.

She and Phoebe wound their way back to the steps.

"This is such a great turnout," Phoebe said. "You'll have a good audience for your first PDX performance!"

"Don't say that!" Shaggy replied. "I just managed to forget that part."

Phoebe grinned wildly. "Aw. Come on. It's gonna be great. And the fact that we might get arrested only makes it better."

"You're determined to freak me out again, aren't you?"

They had reached one of the massive pillars that held up the bridge. Shaggy looked up at the concrete, and past it, the green welded steel. Following the line of steel toward the water, she saw the coiled ropes and silks and the long, rolled-up banners. Everything was staged. They really did need to get up there.

"Not trying to freak you out, trying to get you focused on something other than messing up. It's gonna be great." Phoebe followed Shaggy's line of sight. "Yep. We really need to get up there now. They should be ready to lock down the bridge in another forty minutes or so. That's our signal. The kayaks and boats come after."

"Let's get to it then," Shaggy replied. She swallowed her nervousness and headed up the steps toward the sidewalk that would take them up onto the bridge.

33

MOSS

Moss had just dumped his last load of gear into Tariq's truck when a black, luxury SUV rolled up the street. It was so not the sort of car that belonged up in St. John's. The only wealthy people that rolled through were developers, and the long-term residents hated them. Luxury cars rarely made it out of the neighborhood without getting keyed, or worse.

Moss shaded his eyes with his hand.

"Cover up!" Tariq called to the rest of their crew. "Who the fuck is that?" Tariq asked, flipping an old brown tarp over the gear in the truck bed.

Moss shrugged, still watching. The other activists quickly shut the doors of the perfectly serviceable hatchbacks that looked ancient and battered in comparison to the sleek vehicle creeping up the street. Moss heard the front door of Justice House shut and turned to see Barbara Jean, clad in boots, jeans, and a black denim jacket, standing, arms crossed on the broad porch now emptied of gear. The household's queer pride flag flapped gently in the late morning breeze.

He saw several people twitch, wondering whether to mask up or not. He understood the impulse and hoped they resisted. Masking up this far from an action would mean bad news for everyone involved, and bad news for the neighborhood. Justice House and a few other places already attracted unwelcome notice from the FBI. It was why they no longer held meetings on site. Any attention from the authorities put too many St. John's folks at risk.

The SUV finally stopped when it grew even with Moss and Tariq. A tinted window slid silently down.

It was the woman from the press conference. Patricia Sloane. Her dark hair was down today, but her hectic green eyes looked the same, as did the pale lipstick that framed her white, white, teeth.

"Excuse me." She paused to smile. "Can you tell me how to get to St. John's Bridge?"

Moss froze in place, staring. The sound of water roared inside his ears. Some *thing* anchored to her reached toward him. He barely saw it, a dark gray shimmer. A blot in the bright morning air.

"Never heard of it." He heard Tariq speaking. Good. Someone was speaking. Someone could speak. Gray crowded the corners of Moss's sight. The roaring in his ears grew louder. Blood? Or water? What?

The woman's mouth was still moving. Saying words he couldn't hear. The gray shimmer grew thick. The taste of chemicals flooded his tongue. He swallowed, struggling to not puke. What was she doing to him? Spots danced in his eyes. He needed to get his shields up. Shut down his aura. He couldn't breathe. Drowning. The *thing* swiped, raked across his aura. Marking him. The world went black. Moss felt himself fall, hitting the truck on his way down, hands grabbing him. Shouting.

The screech of a car pulling quickly away.

"Moss! Moss! Someone get me some water!"

Tariq's voice. Then Barbara Jean's.

"What the hell happened? Moss? Honey, come back to us. Did he hit his head again?"

"No. I caught him in time. He whacked his arm pretty good, though."

"Should we move him?"

Moss's eyes fluttered. A sliver of blue sky between Tariq's thin, dark face and Barbara Jean's rounder pale one. The dark gray shimmering was gone. He blinked. Focused. Both his comrades looked worried.

"Hey, Moss. You back?" Tariq waggled a steel bottle in his view. "Want some water?"

"Do you think you can sit up?" Barbara Jean asked.

Moss nodded, then gasped as a sharp pain lanced through his left wrist. Must have clipped it on the truck.

"Fuck," he said, struggling to sit up without using his bruised ribs or putting any pressure on his left hand.

"What's up? What hurts?" Tariq asked, helping to prop him up.

"I messed up my wrist."

Barbara Jean *tsked*. "You know what that means?"

"It means Maggie's going to be happy." It meant there was no way he could lockdown. Dammit. He was so sure....

Then he noticed the roaring in his head was gone. The pressure from the river had subsided. The danger was gone.

"Who was that woman?" Barbara Jean asked as they helped Moss to his feet.

"The woman from GranCo," Moss choked out. *And her egregore.*

"And that's proof enough for me that she had people

stalking you, man. How else she gonna show up on our doorstep like that?" Tariq said.

"We have to warn Terra," Barbara Jean replied. "And get that wrist of yours wrapped. If you're planning on still heading to the park."

Moss snorted. "What do you think?"

They walked Moss toward Justice House.

"Hey Squirrel," Tariq called out. The lanky anarchist ran over.

"What's up?"

"Change in plans. Moss won't be locking down. Can you coordinate the others?"

"Sure. We should be fine with the folks we have. You hurt bad?"

"No. Just borked my wrist. But don't worry, I'll still be there."

Moss felt calm now. No rage. No fear. No worry. Certainty. He knew what he needed to do. He would be there as a witch. As one who spoke to the spirits of place. As an activist.

He would help Raquel face down that egregore.

And thank the ancestors, he wouldn't need to wear a damn diaper to do it.

He'd just wished he'd figured all of this out sooner. He wished the river had let him know the pressure wasn't about locking down, but about facing that woman head on. Because it was clear he was going to need to do that. Whether today or someday soon, Moss and Patricia Sloane were going head to head.

34

SHAGGY

Thinking she could go without her fleece was wishful thinking. Her bare feet were going to be bad enough. Up here on the bridge, small whitecaps below and towering green steel spires above, it was *breezy*. And once they dropped into open space above the water, there was no telling how things would be.

As Terra helped Shaggy get into harness, another person was checking to make sure Phoebe was anchored, and not likely to tangle in the silks. Despite all the practice, Shaggy was nervous.

"You doing okay?" Terra asked. "There's no dishonor in backing out last minute. People do it all the time. I'd rather you said no now than in the middle of the drop."

Shaggy shook out her hands and legs, shaking off the tension and letting the harness settle on her frame as she bounced on the balls of her bare feet. The concrete walkway wasn't too cold, at least.

She looked at Terra, whose hair was secured inside a black head wrap. Practical, given the wind. Shaggy's own hair was short enough to not be much of a problem, but she wished she had a cap to keep the wind from her ears.

"I'm a little scared," she admitted, "but excited, too."

"That's a combination I can live with," Terra said, smiling. "I've gotta go check the banner folks." Terra squared off with Shaggy before leaving. "Just remember, no matter what goes down, we've got you. There's a whole team up here that's going to make sure you keep safe."

Shaggy swallowed and nodded. "Thank you. Just...thanks."

Terra loped off to confer with the activists setting up to drop a massive banner. Shaggy didn't know what it said, and wished she'd thought to ask, but the thing had to be twenty feet wide. She was amazed at this group. It was pretty clear they did this sort of thing all the time.

How, though? Dangling over blue padded mats was one thing. Hanging over rushing water was another. How did someone decide to put themselves on the line, hanging from buildings and bridges while risking arrest at best and plunging to their death at the worst?

They've figured out what's important. The thought came with certainty inside her. *And that's why you're here, isn't it?*

Shaggy felt the truth of it, or at least one piece of the truth. She was here because it *mattered*, even if she wasn't one-hundred-percent sure why. As she stood and stretched, on top of that sunny bridge, it started happening. Three cars blocked the four lanes of traffic. Cars were honking, stacking up behind them. People began to run around like ants, unloading equipment and getting into position.

She scanned the group for Moss's fauxhawk, but didn't see him anywhere. She hoped he was okay.

Phoebe put a hand on Shaggy's arm. "Let's go over the plan one more time. Okay?"

A row of activists began locking themselves into long, white cylinders. Moss wasn't there. He had to be. But he wasn't. What was happening?

"Shaggy? It's time. Let's go over this, okay?"

Shaggy ripped her gaze away, and looked down at the harness and the coils of blue silk, then back to Phoebe's face.

"Okay," she replied. In for a penny, in for a pound.

35

MOSS

Tariq swung beneath the bridge into the tiny, jam-packed parking lot and stopped. Just below, steps led down to the waterfront park that defined the north–south boundary between the Cathedral Park and St. John's neighborhoods, sliced into east–west quadrants by the elegant bulk of the bridge overhead. It looked like the crowd was down by the stage, which meant the blessing ceremony was probably over. Things were right on time.

"I know you're disappointed in the change, but frankly, man, I'm relieved." Tariq looked at Moss from the driver's seat.

"Yeah. I'm kinda sorry now I didn't listen to you all, but..."

"Sometimes you gotta figure shit out your own way."

"Right. That." Moss grinned, then got serious. "Stay safe up there, man. And keep our people safe."

"Safe as I can, but really, you know, that shit all depends on the pigs."

Moss nodded, unbuckled his seatbelt, and leaned over to

give his comrade a side shoulder hug. Old marijuana and Nag Champa incense perfumed his clothes and hair.

"You and the witches stay safe, too. You been hurt enough this past week," Tariq said. Releasing him from the hug, he gave Moss a quick kiss. Moss leaned his forehead against his friend's and sighed, then pulled away.

He slid out of the truck and slammed the door, leaning into the window. "No justice, no peace."

"No justice, no peace," Tariq replied, then, putting the truck in gear, he gave Moss a salute and took off. Moss turned and walked to the top of the concrete stairs leading down to the park. His eyes took in the plum colored leaves of the cherry trees and the huge, golden-leafed maple. The towering firs and scraggly grass. The massive rise of the bridge overhead, and down the gentle hill, past the railroad tracks, the crowd. It looked like a great turnout clustered around the stage area and wandering down near the water. The sound of drums and rattles echoed up the hill as dancers swirled and turned on the small stage.

It was truly a beautiful day out, and warming up a bit, too. A great day for an action. But Moss felt unsettled by his encounter with Patricia Sloane, Environmental Engineer, and it was more than the fact that the encounter had made him black out and re-injure himself. *That* was definitely not good.

He *knew* her, somehow, that woman from GranCo. As soon as she looked at him, he saw her, clearly. He just hadn't realized it in the moment. He'd been too focused on the weird gray shimmer of the egregore.

And now, the river told him more, whispering a vague sense... She and the egregore were connected to the river, just like he was. Everyone who came in contact with the water was connected, but this woman? She paid attention to the river. Her connection was more intimate than the average person who crossed any of the seven bridges every day. Whether she knew it or not, in helping build the egregore, Patricia Sloane worked to affect the river directly, and much as she might want to deny it, she knew that in her soul.

Through the kami of the river, Moss read that in the memory of her, in the image of her eyes burned on his brain.

And this was new, this ability. Some small part of him made a note to tell Brenda and Raquel that his psychic powers were expanding. But for now, he had to let that go, and ride the information flowing through.

He saw Patricia Sloane. He felt her inner drive. Listened to the beat of her ambition. Tasted her fear of being left behind.

Patricia Sloane was a person who had lost her sense of home. She buried her sorrow beneath a bright and brittle anger. And GranCo had used all of this. And the egregore had grown.

A grudging compassion rose inside him, but it still wasn't okay for her to threaten the lives of countless others. Animals. Plants. All the fish that would lose their home. All of the people whose neighborhoods would be affected by the scent of pollution and the sicknesses that followed.

Her pain did not excuse dealing pain out to these others. It never could and never should.

Moss clenched the fist on his uninjured arm, then opened it again. His right hand, the hand of action. His left hand was the hand of magic and intuition. He would need to rely on other, expanded senses, to do that work today. Breathing in the green of the grass and the distant smells of river water and the smoke from burning sage, he rocked his feet on the grass. He sent out a tendril of awareness and greeted the Willamette, and clapped his right hand on his thigh, a courtesy that at this point felt barely necessary, they were so intertwined. Moss smiled and sent out a thank you to the spirit the bridge was named for. The wandering spirit that named the neighborhood Justice House stood upon. The old settler and recluse, a man named James John, who the people came to call the hermit, St. John. A Holy Fool.

"I can use a little of what you had, my friend," Moss murmured to the air. "A little wild wisdom, please. Some foolishness. Let me act outside the ordinary, and do what needs to be done."

He pulled his phone from his pocket and winced.

"Damn. Need to switch pockets." It was almost time for his comrades on the bridge to be getting in place. He needed to find the rest of Arrow and Crescent Coven, especially Raquel and Alejandro. He'd texted them the change of plans but hadn't gotten clear coordinates of where they all would be. The whole coven—minus Brenda and Cassie who had to mind the shop and the café—should arrive at any time.

His left wrist throbbed, and his knee, elbow, and hip were all messed up, along with his ribs. He was a wreck, and yeah, he should've listened to his friends in the first place, before today's psychic smack down.... But he'd been so damn sure the urgency he felt meant that he needed to lock down.

Ego masquerades in many ways. Should've listened more carefully to the river, instead of just going off the emotional energy.

He thumbed another message to Raquel, giving his current location. His eyes swept across the grass, and then down through the massive concrete arches, the outdoor cathedral that held up St. John's Bridge. Closing his eyes, he felt all the heat, pain, and complaining in his tortured tendons and bruised muscles. Acknowledging the pain, he breathed past it. Through it. He inhaled deeply into his belly, letting the park and the people, the scents and the sounds, flow all the way through his being, softening his edges, and opening him to the magic that moved through every living thing.

Then he imagined his breath moving down all the way through the soles of his feet. As he connected to the earth below, he simultaneously reached upward toward the tall green gothic spires of the suspension bridge and further, to the blue autumn sky. He felt the deep, heavy strength of the concrete and the soaring of the steel.

Beneath it all, the river hummed. Moss exhaled, expanding his ætheric bodies, feeling the strength and centered softness every magic worker cultivated. In his right hand, his phone buzzed. He checked the text. *Parking now*.

He could feel it in the energy of the park. A shift, and a barely describable taste on the back of his tongue. The witches had arrived—he felt it the second their feet touched the grass—and overhead, the blockade was almost in place.

And Shaggy was getting ready to go over the edge.

"Thank you," he whispered to the river. Grateful for the knowledge, he turned to greet his friends.

36

SHAGGY

Terra had given her a peppermint, saying it would calm her down. Somehow, sucking on the hard candy actually helped. Whether it was the mint, or the distraction, or some primal comfort that came from the sucking motion, Shaggy couldn't tell. She felt grateful, all the same.

Looking out past the huge steel cables, over the expanse of the river, toward downtown Portland, for the first time in her life Shaggy felt as if every part of her was present. She was filled with an upwelling sense of love. She wished she could kiss Moss before going over the edge, but that wasn't going to happen. Even though she couldn't see him, he had to be busy with the group that had just arrived in a small caravan of cars, and were busy locking themselves to the bridge around thirty feet away. She recognized Moss's friend Tariq, but still no Moss.

Just let Moss be okay.

"You almost ready?" Phoebe asked.

Shaggy looked at the woman who was her teacher and who maybe, just maybe, was becoming her friend. Phoebe's headwrap was barely doing its job of keeping escaped strands of hair from her braid from whipping around her face. Shaggy kicked herself again for not bringing a cap to cover her ears. They were already icy cold.

"Ready as I'll ever be," Shaggy said. "How do we do this?" She flexed her bare toes on the sidewalk, then shook out her legs.

Phoebe smiled. "We climb up on the railing edge, slowly lower ourselves until we've cleared the bridge, and then start dancing."

Shaggy inhaled deeply, shook out her hands and legs again, and rolled her head on her neck. Then she exhaled. *Okay? Okay.*

"Lead the way."

Terra and another woman stepped forward.

"No matter what happens," Terra said, "I want you to remember that we've got you. The harness can hold people twice your weight, it's clipped to solid steel, and both Sam and I are trained as anchors. Okay?"

Shaggy wiped damp palms down her fleece jacket and nodded. She felt an urgent need to pee and hoped it was just nerves, and not anything real, because it was way too late for a bathroom break.

No turning back.

She squeezed Phoebe's hand, gave Terra a thumbs-up, and climbed onto the green metal railing, then over the other side. She drew the blue silks around her hands and in between her thighs, tugged backward on the harness, and felt the rope give her slack, then stabilize.

She looked up at the gothic towers of the bridge and sent up a quick prayer.

Let everyone be safe. She didn't know whom she prayed to, but it felt good to do it, all the same.

Then, bracing her feet against the edge of the bridge,

she pushed outward, felt the rope release, and dropped down over the river, the tail ends of the blue silk billowing in the wind.

37

MOSS

"Brother, you saw the light!" Alejandro threw out his arms and rushed toward Moss as if to engulf him in a giant hug.

Moss jerked back and winced, holding up his hands. "Don't slam me, bro."

Alejandro pulled up short. "Sorry. Right."

The rest of the coven, minus Cassiel and Brenda, had arrived by that point. Raquel looked at him with concern in her brown eyes. She looked ready for battle, the long coils of her dreads tied back in a purple wrap. She also had boots on her feet, wore jeans and a hoodie, and had a bandana ready around her neck in case of police-issued pepper spray. Moss felt a little sad to see that. Raquel had always been badass, but she'd never been this kind of warrior before white supremacists had beaten the shit out of her son and fire-bombed her boyfriend's shop.

Everybody had some turning point when they decided that not only were they not going to take shit anymore, they were willing to deal out actual harm if necessary.

"Did something else happen?" Raquel asked. "Besides

the accident? Something else happened. Damn it. When were you were going to tell us about this one?"

"It seemed better to tell you in person," Moss replied, "rather than freak you out in advance."

"Besides which," Tempest replied, "you knew that several of us would have told you to go home." Her short, white-blond hair spiked out around her head, and her tattooed arms were covered by a black hoodie. Skinny black jeans tucked into bright purple Doc Martin boots completed the outfit.

"It's not that bad," Moss said. "Can we drop the subject now? We have work to do."

"You can't fake out a healer," Tempest said. "It's worse than you're saying."

She jerked her head toward their coven mate Tobias—whose floppy, dark brown hair and goatee both needed trimming. He'd stopped to tie the laces on his sneakers.

Tobias looked up, shook a lock of hair from his eyes, and replied, "Tempest and I saw it in your body the minute we stepped into the park." He stood. "You're holding yourself like you're in pain. Will you let Tempest and I do some work on you before we start?"

"No time. Shit's already going down. Can't you feel it?"

He certainly could. He felt his comrades locking down on the bridge above, he felt Shaggy pushing off the bridge. And he really wanted to see that but didn't know if he'd make it. He felt the boats on the water, and the elders still singing out their prayers. From across the park, the drums sounded again. Tempest huffed impatiently. "Do I at least have permission to send you some energy while we work?"

Moss nodded.

Raquel sniffed the air, and he saw her eyes change. The

hairs stood up on his arms and he pulled his cowl closer around his neck, suddenly chilled.

Raquel nodded. "You're right," she said. "Shit is certainly going down. And some bad shit is on its way."

He could feel that, too. And he didn't like it.

Be like water... The Willamette whispered in his veins.

"Let's do this," he said.

38

SHAGGY

She pushed away from the bridge, felt the harness jerk again, and then she was free. Anchored, yes, but free all the same. Wind caught the silks and blew them straight out from where they wrapped around her thighs. She struggled to right herself as another gust shoved her toward Phoebe and the green silks that whipped and snarled around her teacher's legs. Breath catching in panic, her head swiveled just as Phoebe gave her a brilliant smile.

"You're okay," Phoebe mouthed. Shaggy struggled to breathe normally and decided that whether not she was actually okay, she would decide to just *be* okay.

She rolled herself down the blue silks, getting used to the way the harness held her hips, before arching backwards. *Gotta just trust this, Shaggy,* she thought, and slowly freed the death grip her left hand had on the silk. Exhaling, she moved again, fingertips describing an arc outward, then tracing a pathway down toward the river.

Here goes. She inhaled. Held the breath. Exhaled. Then, closing her eyes, she let her body turn and turn and turn again, the silks grabbing her thighs and calves at each turning. Shaggy turned in the wind until she dangled upside down above the river, cradled by the harness, Terra and the ropes anchoring her above, the soft silks, and the buoyant wind itself.

Wind and water, silk and rope, these were her allies in the dance. She felt enormous, as if her body and soul had tripled in size. As though she could face anything in the world. Opening her eyes, she gasped again, this time in wonder. For down below her on the water was a phalanx of kayakers and sailboats, flags and bright banners rippling in the breeze. Those boats on that river, and the green and blue silk that billowed around her, and the people on the shore dancing and waving...taken all together it was the most beautiful thing she'd ever seen. The most beautiful thing she'd ever felt. And Shaggy knew then that *this* was part of her destiny.

Doing something that mattered, and adding to the beauty of the world. She could do that. She would do that.

It wasn't her father's legacy, or Bianca's. This was going to be Shaggy's own.

She felt the spark of life quickening inside of her, and in that moment—that brave, beautiful, ecstatic moment—she knew with equal certainty that a child was not her destiny. At least not right now. Once this was done, she'd make an appointment. Have an abortion. Set free whatever spirit might have attached itself to her.

And she felt nothing from that thought but a detached peace. And then that thought was gone along with every other thought, and she was simply in her body, winding and unwinding, arcing and swaying, dangling above the vast, powerful river, fighting for something bigger than herself.

Shaggy felt as luminous as the sun. Catching Phoebe's eyes, she smiled, and then laughed until the wind stole her breath away.

39

MOSS

Raquel raced off toward the crowd, Tobias and Lucy frantically trailing after. Their hair and skin shone in the early autumn sun, and if Moss squinted slightly, he could see the further spark of light and movement around Raquel's partially wrapped head. Her Goddess, Yemoja. Good.

But Moss had no time to think of that. His feet itched to move, and the taste of brackish water licked at the base of his tongue.

"Let's walk toward the water. I need to get a sense of things. Just keep me from getting trapped in the crowd, okay?"

Tempest and Alejandro fell into step beside him and slightly behind. The river rose inside him. He felt the fishes and vegetation beneath the surface, and the flying insects and birds of prey that skimmed the surfaces. And the boats. Small craft. Kayaks and sailboats. He felt the breeze from the water. Saw the colors.

All of this was superimposed on top of his physical senses. Sight, sound, scent, the way the grass gave beneath his feet, the way the sun felt on his skin. The burning white sage. The beat of drums. The quick flash of billowing blue and green silk that flowed like quicksilver down toward the water...all of this was present. All of it mattered. But all of it paled beneath the steady rise of river water. The sense of life, teeming, moving, breathing.

The closer his body got to the river, the stronger the sense of dis-ease grew. The more the watery taste in his mouth burned with poison. Oil and chemicals. Waste and the scent of an imminent die out of plants, and fish, and birds, and animals only recently revived.

And he smelled her then. Patricia Sloane. And the egregore. Moss staggered. The threat was real. Here. Now.

"Faster!" he shouted to his friends, and took off running, muscles screaming in pain, left wrist throbbing with heat, pulled by a force so great there was no resisting it.

"Shift left, man." Alejandro's voice penetrated the urgency. Moss veered, and some dim part of his brain just hoped he'd chosen the correct direction. He stumbled and felt Tempest's hand steady him. Catching his footing again, he pounded toward the river as quickly as he could.

Toward the ribbon of water, guided by the autumn sun. Toward the edges of the people, the bright colors and pockets of black. Toward Raquel, shining like a beacon, head on fire with the power of her Goddess. Running toward the source of the poison. He could see her now—Patricia Sloane—with her seal dark hair falling around her shoulders. And the man next to her. And the group of reporters, starting to cluster around. Squinting his eyes, he saw the sickness that surrounded them, rooting its way into their souls. The man was filled with it. Patricia Sloane? The egregore surrounded her like a veil, and he could feel the tendrils of it reaching, seeking, just penetrating the ætheric body that sheathed her skin.

It was an egregore of collective greed. A magical being built by every executive in the company, fed with the demands of every shareholder who never questioned exactly what making all that money cost. Hammered into shape by the will of Patricia Sloane. Maybe she didn't know it, at least not consciously. But she was very, very good at wielding the power of it all the same. Her subconscious was completely taken over by the sense of belonging to the egregore. Directing it gave her life a purpose. It gave her meaning, and a place to belong.

A sense of purpose was a powerful thing.

"Maybe there's a chance," he said, boots pounding on the grass, jeans swishing around his legs. "Maybe there's a chance." The words repeated themselves, over and over, matching the cadence of his running and weaving with the rhythm of the drums. His body screamed its agony, but Moss couldn't stop. "Maybe there's a chance."

His pain was nothing to the pain of the Willamette. His pain was nothing to that of the fish and the trees. His pain was nothing to the neighborhoods of Cathedral Hill and St. John's. His pain was...

"Maybe there's a chance."

The river rose inside him, all life, and light, and poisoned water. The spirit of the river spoke his name.

It knew him. And he knew the river. He ran past Raquel, aware of her, reaching for the egregore. But he couldn't pause to stop. To think. To understand. He ran down to the small wooden pier, toward the glimmering water dotted with flower petals. He climbed over the metal railing, and dove in.

And Moss and the kami of the river were one.

The water held him as if he were a drop of water, submerged within the larger family of droplets, all heading, someday, toward the ocean all water on earth belonged to. He was alive. The river was alive.

He felt oil slick his skin, and felt the chemicals that laced the water. Manifestations of the egregore, meeting the kami of the river. No wonder Patricia Sloane knew the river. She was part of that which poisoned its body. They were intimately entwined.

Moss surfaced.

His eyes took in the boats behind him, and Shaggy, her pale, red-blond hair caught by the sun, silks billowing, dancing with Phoebe, suspended up above his head. Turning, he scanned the crowd on shore, allowing his vision to double again, an old priestess trick of seeing the visible and the ætheric at the same time. He saw the dancing, jostling crowd, the drummers, and the small phalanx of GranCo flunkies surrounded by the press that should have been covering the celebration turned rally....

And, smiling, he knew just what he needed to do. He paddled back toward the wooden pier where Tempest and Alejandro were gathered with a few others, gesturing him to reach up. He did. Tempest and Alejandro pulled him over. He flopped, wet and panting on the weathered wooden slats, stinking of river.

"I need to get up to the top of the bridge."

"What? We just got you out of the river!" Tempest said. "You're in no condition, Moss! Can you even walk a quarter mile uphill right now? Because that's how far it is."

"She's right, brother. Don't be an idiot," Alejandro said. Someone wrapped a blanket around his shoulders, but he felt as if he could burn the water right off his own skin, boiling it into steam. Moss was on fire.

"The press! They're listening to Patricia and…" *And the egregore.* "They're not covering the lockdown! We need to get up top! All the people…they need to get up top. If the dancers can't capture their attention, maybe the lockdown will." The adrenaline that flooded his system made him shake. The taste of brackish water and oil was joined by the taste of spit and copper. The river filled him. All the creatures of the river filled him. He wanted to run. To swim. To fly.

"Now!"

"Okay then," Alejandro said. "Okay. It's going to take a while to get there, though."

"What?" Moss's head swiveled, looking for a way out, a way through. The air was filled with brightness and sound. Confusion. He couldn't…

"We have to get all the way back to Philadelphia Street," Alejandro was saying. "To the pedestrian walkway. And no matter what your spirit is telling you, your body is still injured, Moss."

Moss looked up at the billowing blue and green silks that shimmered above the banners and flags of the kayaks and the boats on the water. He saw Shaggy arch her back and tumble, end over end, before catching herself again. Phoebe followed, spinning and tumbling, green silk to Shaggy's blue. His heart leapt at the sight of it. *This* was the moment. This.

He could feel the prayers that hovered over the surface of the water, blessing everything their sound had touched. The prayers surrounded him, touching him where the water wet his clothes and skin. He just hadn't felt them before.

GranCo's egregore was strong, but not as strong as this. Moss was sure of it.

GranCo didn't matter. They would crumble into dust,

worn down like stone beneath the steady pressure of water. They would crumble beneath the force of the river and the will of the people that the waters run clean.

The salmon and the cormorants would always have a home.

"We will tell the city, now, in public. Raquel will speak. I will speak. Kiyiya will tell the truth about who these people are, and what they are." The words tumbled across Moss's lips as though he were in a trance. "But we must speak from the top of the bridge. Lure the press away from GranCo. Let the rest of the city know what's really going on."

As above, so below.

"Let me call Tobias. Get word to Raquel and...what was the other name?" Tempest asked.

"Kiyiya."

"What should I tell them?"

"That the shitheads from GranCo are here and we need to tell the city to break the goddamn contract. People need to jam the phone lines, send emails, whatever.... But I gotta go. Now."

The egregore had something planned. Moss didn't know what it was but he could feel it in his aching bones and on his damp skin. It was more than making nice with politicians and the press, though Patrician Sloane did that job very well. The egregore had been built simply to make money, but had morphed into something even worse. Poisoning the river fed its power. Doing things the right way slowed it down. It was determined to pick up speed. Destruction fed profits. Profits fed the joy of the shareholders. Their joy fed the egregore's oil-slicked belly.

Moss flung the blanket from his body and stumbled as he tried to rise. Alejandro wrapped one strong arm around him and helped him upright until they were both standing again.

His body trembled. Adrenaline and the cold shock of the water had flushed out the pain—at least temporarily. He needed to keep moving. To follow the course the water whispered in his blood. To fulfill his sacred task.

"I'll go with him," Alejandro was saying to Tempest. "You follow us as soon as you get ahold of Tobias or Raquel. We'll meet you up there."

And then Moss was running. He heard Alejandro curse, then follow. Moss's socks squished inside wet boots, the grass parted beneath his feet. The crowd moved like an elegant serpent, shifting out of their way. Breath screamed hot into his tortured lungs as he wound through people, grass, and trees. Alejandro passed him, clearing the way, running toward the sidewalk that would take them to the top of the bridge.

Moss had never run so fast in his life. His bones jarred at the sudden switch from grass to concrete. He heard Alejandro, breath as even as his gait. Horns honked from stopped cars. Wheezing, he crested the bridge and saw Tariq's truck up ahead, and the other cars in the convoy, blocking the lanes. As he got closer to the obstruction he saw his comrades, two of them chained by the waist, locked to either side of the great expanse, chained to the line of black clad people sitting on tarmac, arms chained inside long white tubes. He saw his friends passing out fliers to the cars with open windows, explaining what was going on. He saw an arc of white spit hit a dark cheek, and a red handkerchief wipe away the moisture, before his comrade walked away. Further down the sidewalk, he saw Terra and her cohort anchoring the harnesses holding Shaggy and Phoebe.

And watching it all, the gothic spires with their mighty,

welded plates of green metal rose like sentinels upward, to the sky.

Moss inhaled, buffeted by a breeze that was much stronger up here than in the sheltered park below. He slowed his run, the aches in bones and muscles returning. His bruised ribs caught at his lungs on every breath. The soles of his feet tingled with pins and his left wrist was on fire.

But Moss didn't care. He felt the cars. The river surging below. The dancer's prayers. He felt the strength of his comrades, and the people, and the beauty of the day.

In the midday sunlight, there on top of St. John's Bridge, Moss felt the balancing point, the equinox, as it came to rest inside him.

For the first time in his life, Moss knew that he was whole.

40

SHAGGY

Moss. Shaggy's heart flew into her throat. She coughed and gulped at the wind. Phoebe was signaling to her, but she couldn't pay attention. She'd seen him dive into the water. Had he surfaced? *Why* wasn't he up on the bridge?

The rope tugged at her harness. Damn it. She grabbed at the rope, her hands slipping on the silks, she struggled to right herself again. To begin the climb back to the bridge.

What the hell is going on?

She didn't know. She couldn't know. Shaking her head, Shaggy narrowed her focus to her hands, gripping the rope. To her thighs and knees, grabbing and re-twining themselves around the silks. No matter what was happening below, Shaggy had to get back up top. Falling into the water wouldn't help anyone. Wouldn't help Moss. And who knew what that crazy witch was doing, anyway. He was supposed to be up on the bridge, not canyoning off a wooden dock into frigid water.

The sense of freedom she had felt was gone. It was hard, climbing in the open air. A lot more difficult than the descent. Descending, it didn't matter much if the wind caught silk and swung you off course. Gravity was on your side. Battling wind and gravity at the same time wasn't something she'd ever had to do before. This climb took all her effort. Sweat rolled down her back and sides.

Muscles burning, she heaved herself upward, wind battering her face, hands freezing despite the sweat. And there it was. A lug nut like a huge green eye before her, its cousins rising up the steel in one straight line. Marking the path. She gasped in a huge breath, lungs working like a bellows, muscles shaking with effort.

Shaggy's feet pushed off from metal. Her left hand grasped the metal rail. Strong hands gripped her beneath her arms and yanked her up. Ribs and breasts crashing into metal, Shaggy tumbled over and onto the concrete walkway. Her butt landed with a bruising thump, cracking her teeth together. She fought to slow down her breathing and fight her way out of the silks.

"You're good, girl. You're good." Terra. Hovering around her. Unclipping the harness. Untangling the top and silk.

The solid ground felt good. Familiar. But she already missed being cradled by the wind. And...

"Moss! He jumped into the water!"

"Someone else will take care of him. We're taking care of you, now." Terra raised her head and called out, "Can we get a blanket? Water?"

Boots slapping concrete. A voice. "Here you go." Soft warmth enveloped Shaggy. Water bottle under her nose.

"Drink something," Terra said.

Shaggy drank. The water was good. Really good. She gulped more down, wishing it was tea. Or a shot of whiskey. Yeah. She was *really* cold.

Cars started honking further down the bridge, around the blockade. Voices shouted.

"What the—?" Terra said.

Shaggy stood, trembling, still halfway tangled in the silks. She swayed, and Terra caught her.

Shaggy went up on the balls of her feet. She needed to *see*. On the other side of the lockdown, running, limping, one arm wrapped around his waist.... It was Moss. A soaking wet Moss. He was safe.

But even from a distance, his eyes looked different.

They were black as the bottom of a well.

41

MOSS

There were people. Shouting. Cars. Honking. No police. So strange. Surely someone had called this in by now.

He ran up to Tariq, who gesticulated, deep in conversation with Squirrel. Tariq's head snapped up as Moss got closer.

"Moss! What happened to you, man?"

Moss stopped and bent over, hands on his knees, breath wheezing in and out. Damn it. Every part of his aching body was on fire now and his ribs and wrist were killing him. It was as if he'd never been dunked in the icy water at all.

Except that, underneath the adrenaline and pain, the river still flowed steadily through his veins.

"He jumped in the river," Alejandro said. "Idiot. And then ran all the way up here."

Moss ignored both of his friends. He needed to catch his breath, but the magic rolled through him, making it hard to do anything except lie down on the bridge. He felt the kami strengthening, aided by Raquel and her Goddess, ready to meet the egregore head on. Moss felt ready, too. Ready to enter the æthers again. Ready to face the poison, the greed and the lies.

He wasn't the best trained person in the coven, but he knew the river, and the river knew him. Moss sensed the GranCo egregore creeping around the edges of his consciousness, assessing the enemy, trying to get in. Well, it wasn't going to.

"Alejandro!" he gasped out. "Protection. Around me."

"You got it."

Moss felt the air around him thicken, growing more palpable. He nodded, then receded back into his thoughts, seeking out the taste of magic and the work that needed to be done.

The egregore was built for one purpose only: to make money, by any means necessary. To make money and to delude those who might ask how or why. But that was only the beginning of its life. As it grew, the spirit of GranCo decided, deep in its sick little magical child brain, that it wanted more power. How to get that power?

By controlling shareholders and executives alike. By increasing the influx of capital and the output of the poisons that ensured the money would flow, no matter what.

And then? By choking the river until everything within it began to die. Then there would be no worries about environmental impact. No more struggle with pretending to keep the waters clean.

Distant drumming mixed with the honking of the cars. Moss smiled. The people were coming. In one long procession, they walked and danced and rolled their way up the bridge. They crowded the sidewalks, they danced between the cars. Feathers shook and rattles sounded. Ribbons and fringed shawls danced through the air. And above it all, bright banners announced to the world that Water is Life, that the Willamette Must Run Clean. Painted fish swam beneath cardboard birds, held aloft by adults and children alike.

The party had arrived.

As the crowd came closer, Moss closed his eyes, dropped his attention into his solar plexus, and *listened*, with all his might. He heard the silent prayers of the elders. Felt the GranCo egregore battling with the mighty Raquel, who wielded the power of Yemoja, she of rivers and oceans. She whose power would not be denied. He heard the kami of the Willamette, calling out his name.

And then he heard what the people were chanting, a vibrant call and response, and he threw back his head and laughed.

"The waters of life are rising up! The waters of life will drown all greed! The waters of life run sweet and clean! The waters of life are all we need!" Over and over, the chant looped, and swam, and soared. Tariq picked it up on the bullhorn microphone and began to chant with them.

"The waters of life are rising up!" Tariq sang.

"The waters of life will drown all greed!" the people replied.

"The waters of life run sweet and clean!"

"The waters of life are ALL WE NEED!"

The people had reached the lockdown. News cameras and reporters shoved their way through cars and crowd. Kiyiya walked forward, dark eyes darting between Moss and Tariq. The drums pounded, and the chant swirled, faster and faster, until the lead drummer raised his stick, high in the air, and as if all the drummers were one body, and one drum, a booming echo rolled across the bridge. Three strikes upon the skins.

Boom! Boom! Boom!

Kiyiya raised his hands. Slowly, silence spread from the front of the crowd to the back. Tariq held the mic of the bullhorn up to Kiyiya's mouth.

"The waters of life must run clean!"

Every camera was trained on Kiyiya, and the backdrop of the locked down anarchists. They'd gotten one of the large "Water is Life" banners to the other side of the lockdown, where it formed a backdrop for Kiyiya to stand in front of. Moss smiled. In the dim recesses of his mind he knew that this was good messaging, and good theater. Everything needed to capture imaginations that would otherwise never pay attention to what was going on under their noses as they went about their lives.

But most of Moss's consciousness was with the kami of the river. He felt a hand on his shoulder, and smelled the familiar scent of lilac. Shaggy. And on the other side of him, a solid presence, smelling slightly of mint. Terra.

"I might need you to hold me up," he said. "I'm going under, and I'm going fast."

"I don't know what you're talking about," Terra replied, "but whatever you need, I'm here."

"Me, too." Shaggy's voice was soft next to his ear. "Go with the river, Moss. We're here. And I love you."

She loves me... High up on the bridge, the waters closed over Moss's head.

Then Moss was flying, buoyed by etheric waters, up to the astral planes.

42

SHAGGY

The east side of the bridge was filled with people and cars as far as Shaggy could see. Fish and birds, banners and dancers. And one of the elders, saying something into the microphone that Shaggy couldn't focus on long enough to even make out.

Her attention was on the man in front of her. On the heat of his body beneath the damp T-shirt. Like hanging upside down above the waters of the Willamette, standing beside Moss, facing whatever might come, felt right to her.

But that sense of rightness didn't ease her worry.

Something was wrong with Moss. Very wrong. But strangely, he also felt more himself, somehow. Despite the fact that she could barely feel him in his body, she somehow knew that, just as she had felt her destiny while dangling off the side of this bridge, Moss's destiny was unfolding around them all, right here. Right now.

"We've got you, Moss," she whispered again. "Just let go."

She looked at Alejandro, who gave her a nod, but said nothing, face set in a mask of concentration.

And then Moss began to speak. He lifted his arms in a

mirror of Kiyiya, who was still speaking on the bullhorn mic box. Moss's words were soft at first, growing louder with each utterance.

"There is poison in the water. There is poison in their hearts. There are mirrors, mirrors everywhere. Look! Look now! And never look away again." His body swayed with the rhythm of his words. She and Terra kept a hand upon each shoulder, making sure he didn't fall. It was funny: just moments ago, it had felt as if Shaggy could barely stand, but in this moment? Nothing could move her.

Kiyiya turned and said something to Tariq, who nodded, then moved to stand next to Moss, holding the square mic box in front of his mouth.

"We think that evil doesn't walk here, with us. We think that this is the twenty-first century, and such language only belongs in the past. But together, we can create powerful community, and beauty, and together, we can flow with the river, bringing justice. Bringing change. But just as surely as we can do those things, humans can also create monsters out of our greed or helplessness. And that greed poisons soil and sky. And water."

The words climbed their way up Shaggy's spine, settling in the space between heart and throat. She was a little freaked out by this Moss-Not-Moss person who was speaking. Touching him, feeling the vibration of words through skin, felt alien. Strange. Her mind wanted to reject all of it as ridiculous—his words, and the fact that the man she knew as Moss wasn't exactly speaking right now—but her heart knew otherwise. She could feel the poison he was speaking of. She knew the sense of hopelessness, and had brushed up against that kind of greed. It had tainted her mother and their relationship, though Shaggy didn't think it had swallowed her mother whole.

Not yet, anyway.

But this evil Moss was talking about? It was a swallow-cities-whole kind of thing. Shaggy felt it in her bones.

"There are people here today who would poison our whole city and call it good. They were holding a press conference in the park, just moments ago. Ah." He looked at something in the distance, across the cars and the crowd. Shaggy tracked his gaze past the lockdown and the news crews, toward a cluster of painted cardboard birds and fish. There were people in suits there, looking out of place. "Patricia Sloane. I see you."

Shaggy saw a dark-haired woman in a suit look up. Saw her skin grow pale, her lips set in a thin, grim line. Even from a distance, Shaggy saw a sheen of sweat on the woman's face despite the mildness of the day.

"You profit as you choke our waters, and poison the children, the animals, the trees. My people, Patricia here works for GranCo, and everyone here in this city is paying them. But the river thinks that it is time for them to pay. Time for you to pay, Patricia."

It was as if a ripple moved through the whole crowd. As if something large had just washed over everyone on the bridge, whether bystanders stuck in traffic, or the people who had gathered to bless the river and confront the people intent on harm.

The dark-haired woman raised one hand to shield her eyes. Shaggy looked at Moss, who was still speaking, eyes fixed on the woman, as if engaged in silent battle.

From somewhere in the middle of the crowd, a voice shouted. "GranCo out! The *river* is *sacred*! GranCo out! The *river* is *sacred*!"

Words still flowed from Moss's mouth, but they were washed away by the power of the crowd.

Shaggy shivered in the autumn sun, and the bridge began to shake.

"What's happening?" she called to Terra.

"The cops," Terra replied. "That's the sound of their boots, running up the bridge."

The crowd roared again. Tariq took up the chanting, bellowing it into the bullhorn mic. Fish and birds and banners waved in the air. Cars honked. The people beat their own feet on the bridge.

No longer on the mic, Moss still stared and murmured. Shaggy strained to catch his words.

"The river will protect its own. You, Patricia, you can hide no more."

The small hairs stood up on the back of Shaggy's neck. What the hell was happening here?

"GranCo out! The *river* is *sacred!*" The crowd jostled, danced, and chanted to the beating of the mighty drums. Cameras whirred. And a row of police in riot gear appeared at the far edge of the crowd.

Shaggy began to weep from the strange beauty of it all, or maybe out of fear. She couldn't tell.

For the first time in her life, the two things didn't seem to cancel each other out. Maybe this was what it could feel like to simply be alive.

Maybe this was what it felt like to show up as yourself, and know you mattered.

43

MOSS

He was on the bridge, facing a bright crowd. He was in the river, flowing south. He was in concrete and steel. He was in the sky, tethered to a cloud drifting by. He was in the æthers, high on the astral planes.

Moss danced. Moss swam. Moss was the Willamette and the St. John's Bridge. Moss was the people. Moss was a man.

Moss was a witch in battle, joined with the power of his sister, Raquel, connected, heart to heart, to every member of Arrow and Crescent coven.

High up on the astral, and walking between worlds, as the words of the river poured through him, Moss fought the egregore. Moss fought Patricia Sloane.

The egregore was made of light and sound. A being fed by money, toxins, and blood. A being that cared for nothing. A cancer that cared only for *more*.

But Moss had more than enough. He had a triangle supporting him. Shaggy. Terra. Alejandro. He had Raquel, the river, and the crowd. But most importantly, they all had one another. The monster that he faced would never have that. It had to grow too large because otherwise? It would always die alone.

Alejandro fed Moss a solid skein of energy, gathered from the coven, amplified by the power of the crowd. It moved through Moss's wrists into his fingertips. He was dimly aware of an aching in his left wrist, but it wasn't quite enough to pull him from the æthers and back into his body. He linked with Raquel, sent her a questioning thread.

::*Look*:: she said. ::*Stop focusing on the earth planes and look.*::

Moss dragged his dual attention all the way up and focused. He saw it then, so clearly. On the astral plane, the monster looked like an oil slick surrounding an open, sharp-toothed mouth. It smelled like one thousand board rooms, and ten billion dollar bills. Raquel stood on the other side of the being, conch shell in one hand, wand in the other, sketching patterns in the air. Moss heard it roar inside his head.

"Hey!" he shouted. "Over here!" The egregore turned, and roared again, its breath like burning oil fields. It raked a limb outward again, battering at his shields. Moss hissed as the monster connected with the rips in his aura. The rips it had made when Patricia Sloane had looked him in the eye at Justice House. Up on the astral plane, Moss stumbled, then righted himself again.

Moss didn't care. The egregore had already injured him. It had broken his car. Put him into the hospital. Dashed his body against a truck. It wasn't going to hurt him anymore.

Not today. Not if he could help it.

He reached for the power of the coven, and with one mighty breath, sent their collective power circling the edges of his aura. The mighty rips stitched themselves together. Another pull, another breath, and Moss's aura pulsed with light. The power of the equinox was all around him. And all of a sudden, Raquel was at his side. His mother. His sister. His mentor.

Moss reached for the Willamette. He reached for the power and comfort of the crowd. He reached for Arrow and Crescent Coven. Moss clapped his hands three times. The oil slick jerked with each retort across the astral. It clacked its many teeth, chittering its rage.

At his side, Raquel threw back her head and laughed.

And, up on the astral plane, Moss began to dance. He danced for the fish and the birds and the trees. He danced for the river and the children of St. John's and Cathedral Park. He danced for Shaggy, and the coven, and himself. He danced up magic. He danced up possibility. Moss bounced to the drumming, shouting tempo of the crowd on the bridge. Moss danced to the humming sounds of the astral planes. Moss raised his arms and shook his hands to the music of his own soul.

Raquel and Moss both danced. The power of the river was strong.

Down on the bridge, his physical ears half heard, half felt as the crowd began to roar. He roared with them, as he danced. Every scrap of power he had, everything Alejandro fed him, he channeled toward the sharp-toothed maw.

Feed your demons. The thought flicked through his brain. An old magical teaching, found in among magicians in old Europe, and taught by Buddhists in Tibet. *Feed them what they* need. *Not what they want.*

::*Feed the demon, Raquel!*::

::*What?*::

What this demon, this egregore, this being, wanted was to consume everything alive. What this being *needed* was to feel a part of things. Just like Patricia Sloane. It needed to know that it was one piece of a beautiful, shining whole.

He sent that feeling to Raquel. She nodded and held out her hands, feet still moving in the patterns of her dance. The conch shell in her right hand re-appeared. From the mouth of the shell flowed healing waters. Healing for the egregore. Healing for the people. Healing for the waters of life.

Moss danced, and wept, and held out his own hands, feeding the egregore knowledge. Feeding the egregore acceptance. Feeding the egregore love. Feeding the egregore a way home.

The being thrashed and fought, and gnashed its teeth. It changed shape, morphing from a diffuse, amorphous blob, into a triangle, then a flame, then back into a vast, shimmering lake.

Moss clapped three more times. The power pumping through him escalated, increasing in power until the edges of his aura trembled with it. His head roared with power. The egregore roared back. Moss felt every molecule inside his physical and astral bodies shake, on the verge of breaking apart. But the egregore wasn't done with him yet. It still *needed*, though its wants were growing less.

"Take it!" His voice boomed across the astral planes. "Take it all!"

With a mighty draw, he threw everything Alejandro was feeding him, every scrap from the coven and the crowd. The being shrieked and whooshed, folding in on itself in some strange geometry. Eating itself with its own mouth. Becoming something new.

Raquel poured out a steady stream of love. Moss felt it. It was strong.

He shattered in a burst of energy and light, one with the

cosmos. One with the planets. The stars. The earth. One. One. One.

He felt hands on his physical body. Jerked back, head pounding. Screaming. Heard a woman's voice, whispering frantically in his ear.

Then all went black.

Moss was pulled back under. Back into the river. Cradled. Surrounded. Lifted by dark water.

The Willamette River blessed every particle named Moss. Somewhere, somewhen, two hands clapped three times.

44

—————

SHAGGY

Moss fell, caught by Shaggy and Terra. Alejandro helped ease him to the ground. His eyes moved and jumped beneath his closed eyelids as if he was dreaming. As Terra checked his pulse, Shaggy looked up to see what was happening.

She saw Patricia Sloane stumble, then collapse, grabbed by two men in suits.

Then the police were everywhere, and a mechanical voice warned the crowd to disperse.

"How the fuck are they supposed to disperse when cops are blocking the only exit?" Terra muttered. "Moss, you're gonna have to come back to us." She turned to Alejandro. "We need to get him the fuck out of here."

Shaggy leaned over Moss. He still didn't look right. Hair damp from the river, skin sallow. At least his eyes had stopped jumping around.

"Moss," she said. "Come back to us. We need you."

With a heaving breath, he coughed, and his eyes flew open.

"We did it," he said.

"That's great, hermano. But now we have to get you on your feet." Alejandro wrapped his arms around Moss, and gently lifted him until he was sitting up. Terra pressed a water bottle up to his lips.

A sawing sound filled the air. The fire department, cutting through the tubes and chains. As each tube was cut, cops stepped in and dragged the locked-down activists away. They were clearing the bridge. Trying to get traffic moving again.

Shaggy, Alejandro, and Terra hoisted Moss up and half-dragged, half-walked him toward the west side of the bridge. It wasn't the best place to take a barely there person who needed who knew what kind of attention, but the only other way off the bridge was through the cops and the crowd.

There was no way would they have made it.

Moss swayed and mumbled, but at least his feet were moving. Sort of.

Alejandro and Terra did most of the dragging and carrying, and put Shaggy in charge of humping Terra's messenger bag and using Alejandro's phone to text the coven and tell them what was up. Her heart was pounding, sure some cops would run up on them at any moment. Glancing over her shoulder, she saw that they were still occupied. Shaggy exhaled.

"Is he going to be okay?" she asked Alejandro. Moss was still sallow and pale, and did not look good at all.

"He'll probably have a raging headache along with his other injuries. He just needs quiet, and some electrolytes. Maybe some protein. Mostly, he's going to need a lot of sleep. We just need to get him home."

"But that's the other direction..."

"Yeah. No kidding." He struggled to get his phone out, handed it to her. "Text Cassiel. They're usually slow on

Saturday afternoons. Maybe she can get someone else to close the café and come get us. Take us across a different bridge, back to St. John's."

Shaggy found the contact and thumbed a message into Alejandro's phone, alerting whoever this Cassiel was.

Moss stumbled hard and Terra crashed into Shaggy, who barely kept hold of Alejandro's phone.

"How much further 'til we can set him down?" Terra asked.

"We're almost off the bridge," Alejandro said. "After that, we can set him down for a few minutes. Catch our breath. But we're probably going to need to walk him down to a safe intersection so someone can pick us up."

"Is there an intersection nearby?"

"I don't think so. But I'm not sure what else we're gonna do."

His phone buzzed in Shaggy's hand as the bridge began to slope toward the exit. *I'm on my way. Forest Park Trailhead?*

"She's asking about a Forest Park Trailhead," Shaggy said.

"Right!" Terra said, struggling to adjust Moss's arm around her shoulders. He kept slipping, though his color was coming back a little, which Shaggy figured must be good. "I forgot. There's a parking lot there."

"Stop," Moss whispered. "Need water."

Shaggy looked back up the sidewalk. Cars were coming toward them now. The blockade must be cleared. No one else was on the walkway on this end of the bridge.

"Walkway looks clear," she said. "I think we're okay to stop for a minute."

Terra and Alejandro leaned Moss against the side rail and Terra gestured at the messenger bag slung over Shaggy's shoulder.

"My water bottle's in there."

Shaggy flipped the bag forward and rummaged around past medical supplies, energy bars, and an apple. There it was. A turquoise steel bottle. She grabbed it and unscrewed the top before handing it over to Moss.

He could barely hold it. Alejandro caught the bottle before it slipped.

"Let me help you."

Moss drank, eyes closed, then pushed the bottle away with a sigh.

"Water," he said, then gave a little smile. "Water's good. I jumped in the river." His eyes opened on that last, as if he were surprised. His dark eyes caught Shaggy's.

"And you. I saw you. Dancing. You were beautiful. And you told me something...."

Within the protective cage of her ribs, Shaggy's heart beat. She reached out and touched his face.

"We've got to get you off the bridge, Moss." Alejandro interrupted the moment. "Cassiel is coming to take you home. Okay?"

"Okay," Moss replied, eyes never leaving Shaggy's. She leaned in for one careful kiss, then backed away. Taking the water bottle from Alejandro, she screwed the lid on, and slipped it back into the messenger bag.

Terra and Alejandro helped Moss wrap his arms around their shoulders again.

"Shaggy?" Moss asked.

"I'm right here, Moss. I'll be right here until we get you home."

She would, too. She knew some things about herself now, that she hadn't known before the beginning of this week.

She was stronger than she thought she was.

She had her own talents and could make her own way if she needed to.

She seemed to be in love with this weird, gorgeous man.

She could do things that mattered in this world.

And the world was worth trying to save.

45

MOSS

The day after equinox, at the cusp of the year, when dark met light, and day met night. The time of dusk.

It had been a sunny day, gorgeous out, but it was evening now, and Moss was already tired of standing up. He'd slept like the dead for more than fifteen hours. The last thing he remembered was Shaggy, tucking him into bed, a furrow in between her pale eyebrows, lips narrow, trying to smile.

In the gathering evening, Moss stood outside the jail with most of the coven, his housemates minus Barbara Jean, who'd gotten arrested, and a small group of other activists. They'd kept the arrestees in over night, and then most of the day, which was bullshit. But, now that news was out about GranCo and how they'd been shafting the city while taking taxpayer money...there was a good chance local pressure would force the city council to drop charges. If GranCo's contract hadn't already been cancelled, it was going to be, that was for sure. The local media had put the city on blast for ever hiring them and at least two city council members were up in arms.

Turns out GranCo had a record up in Washington State,

and the city council should have known that. Instead, they had trusted the mayor, who had gone to college with Bradley Titus, the GranCo CEO, back in the day. Bastard.

He tapped the bouquet of purple irises against his thigh. Shaggy said she'd show up here, but there were no guarantees. Seeing him like he'd been yesterday? That would freak any normal person out. He just had to hope Shaggy wasn't normal. He didn't think she was, but you never knew. She could decide to turn tail and run back to Marin County, leaving the off-kilter Asian witch behind.

"You okay, brother?" Alejandro asked.

"Yeah. Just...still a little out of it. I'll be fine."

Alejandro squeezed his shoulder and walked off to confer with Raquel and Tempest, leaving Moss to his thoughts.

Moss would hate it if Shaggy did. Still glowing from yesterday's experience on the astral, body still hurting from a week's worth of abuse, he knew half of him was still communing with the kami on the astral planes. But the other half of him? Knew he wanted Shaggy. Wanted to wake up next to her. To go for long bike rides. To dance. To read books together.

He wanted someone besides his housemates to care when he got arrested. Even though he couldn't imagine himself living in her swank condo, or her bunking down at Justice House, he hoped they'd have time to figure that stuff out.

"Moss." He turned. There she was, in blue jeans, fancy sneakers, and a pale green sweater, short strawberry-blond hair shining, eyes seeking out his, wondering if he was actually there.

He leaned in. She leaned in. They kissed, warm and soft, increasing pressure before breaking away again.

"These are for you," he said, handing her the bouquet.

"Irises. They're beautiful. Thank you. How are you? You had me a little freaked out, you know."

"I know. I'm still a little...out there," he admitted, "but I'm going to be fine."

She shaded her eyes and looked toward the jail. "Any word?"

"They should be out soon. Within the next half hour." But he didn't want to talk about his comrades. Didn't want to talk about the action. Not right now.

"Shaggy? I know it's too early to say this, and I know you don't know what's going on with the kid and all that, but..."

"Actually, I decided while hanging upside down over the river. I'm not keeping it."

"Oh. Okay then. Um...can I go with you? When you do whatever procedure you've decided on?"

She gave him a half smile. "That'd be great, Moss. Thank you. But you were about to say something else?"

Right. Here we go. He swallowed. Placed his hands on Shaggy's arms, lightly, so she knew he was there, but could easily get away. If she wanted to. Needed to. She moved in closer, and he wrapped his arms around her in a hug. Her small, strong arms circled his waist, and her cheek rested against his chest.

"I know it's soon, but after everything... Up there on the bridge, right before the cops showed up... I don't know if this'll make any sense to you but, I was up halfway between earth and the astral planes...I went totally still inside, for just one moment, and I knew, Shaggy. I just knew. I knew my magic. And I knew the river. And I knew my coven..."

"And?" He felt her shift and tense up in his arms. Waiting.

He leaned back just far enough to see her beautiful bare

face. He looked into her blue eyes and ran a hand through her short strawberry-blond hair.

"I knew that I love you."

They breathed together for three silent seconds before Shaggy broke the silence.

"You must not remember, but up there on the bridge? I said I love you, too."

"You did?"

"I did."

Thank all the spirits, everywhere. Moss smiled and they kissed again.

A cheer came from all around them. Moss looked toward the entrance. The first of their comrades walked through the glass doors, out into the westering sun.

"They're out!" Moss smiled. "Think you can stand hanging out with my coven and housemates for a while? I promise I'll make it up to you later."

"Well, as long as you promise," Shaggy said, "let's go."

They turned, arms wrapped around each other's waists. His coven waited, smiles on their faces, fisted hands in the air. Moss and Shaggy joined them, just as Barbara Jean and the others raised their fists in answer. Someone started blasting music—The Coup. Moss and Shaggy laughed. Tariq slapped Barbara Jean into a hug. And everyone on the sidewalk started dancing.

Just like the city of Portland, his comrades, his housemates, and Arrow and Crescent Coven were his home. And it seemed like Shaggy might want to be, too. The rich girl, poor boy stuff? He bet they'd figure it out somehow. Together.

He was a very, very fortunate man.

The kami spoke to him.

And a river ran through his veins.

T. THORN COYLE

AUTHOR OF THE PANTHER CHRONICLES

BY DARK

THE WITCHES OF PORTLAND

BOOK EIGHT

BY DARK

Alejandro, phone in hand, earbuds in, paced the sidewalk in front of Charlie's store. A supple, black leather jacket was thrown over his usual pressed black slacks and lightly starched lavender dress shirt. A gray and black checked scarf wound around his neck, warding off the late October chill.

He barely heard the voice on the other side of the phone. He was in crisis. It was an internal crisis, but it was throwing every part of his life into upheaval.

Maybe it was a mid-life crisis? He was forty-five years old, smack in the middle of what he hoped would be a very long, fulfilling life. Really fulfilling. He had a great part-ner--the sexy Shekinah--a great coven, and plenty of money. But life still felt like crap. So here he was, pacing on a sidewalk, trying to ignore the droning, entitled voice yammering in his ear.

He'd much rather be inside. Charlie's gaming store--Owlbear--was his niece and nephew's favorite place to go on their afternoons together. He would pick them up at school and they'd walk the three blocks together, chattering at him about one hundred and ten things, all as quickly as possible. Both of them were talkers, which was funny, because they were also big bookworms. Alejandro had been a bookworm—still was—but leaned toward the decidedly quieter end of the spectrum.

The afternoon edged toward twilight. Alejandro loved the sun, but this year? He welcomed the coming winter, with its long, dark nights. It just felt...restful. He needed some rest.

Just as the year leaned halfway between autumn and winter, the neighborhood was in the midst of a transition, too. There was still some light industrial on the main drag here, with old homes on the side streets, but more and more, small commercial shops like Charlie's mixed with swank new cocktail bars and artisan pizza places alongside tire shops and seedy old bars. It was going the way of all Portland neighborhoods west of 82.

Gentrification, Moss would say. Alejandro didn't mind it as much as some of his more radical coven mates. Alejandro was a fan of nice restaurants and bourgeois bars, though he'd been known to set foot inside the occasional dive. He just wished gentrification didn't come at such a high cost.

What the city needed was rezoning...

Earbuds in, phone in hand, he barely heard the voice squawking in his ear. "I understand," he murmured. Polite noise to keep the person on the line at bay. He watched his nephews[change to nephews from niece and nephews throughout.] appear and disappear in between the window displays packed with board games, toys, and action figures. Deeper inside the store, he knew, were the coveted Magic cards and painted role playing miniatures locked inside a clear glass case. He was supposed to be enjoying their excitement. Buying them an add on pack for their decks, or whatever it was they wanted this week.

Instead, here he was, dealing with this person—rapidly becoming an asshole who wouldn't take no for an answer—on the phone.

"As I stated in my email, I am currently closed to new clients." He was currently closed to *all* clients, but this jerk didn't need that information.

Taking a break. Getting his head together. Or whatever the hell he was supposed to be doing.

Maybe he was depressed. Was he depressed? He didn't feel like it. He just felt...alternately numb and frustrated.

Alejandro looked across the street to the low slung building that housed Sub Rosa, the Mexican American food place. They served up a decent margarita. Maybe he'd take the kids for tacos. The food carts down the street were more auténtico, but it was a little too chilly to eat outside today and he just didn't feel like crowding into the brightly lit, boisterous indoor eating space.

Then he remembered. The offrendas should be up. Maybe he'd take the kiddos there after all.

"I have another call coming in. I'm sorry. I need to go. But if you want a referral..."

The guy actually hung up. Good thing, because no way was Alejandro referring this asshole to anyone he trusted anyway. He had to stop with the polite noises.

"Fucking Spic!" a voice yelled out from a car speeding past. Alejandro flipped a middle finger at the receding bumper.

"Pendejo," he said, without too much heat in it. The coven and the rest of the community had dealt a big blow to the white supremacists, but that didn't mean the assholes weren't still around.

He shoved his phone into his jacket pocket, ran a hand across the stubble on his head, and sighed. He should get inside. Let the kids pull him into their excitement. But he just wasn't ready. Couldn't shake the sense of wrongness that had crept forward in his consciousness for the last six months, finally coming to a head around the equinox.

It was guys like the jerk on the phone––and the asshole in the car–– who'd led to Alejandro's current crisis. Right now? He questioned everything he'd worked so hard for. All the training. All the hours. All the money in his bank account. It all felt tainted now. Badly fought for, badly won.

He watched people smoking outside one of the dive bars across the street. Sometimes he wished he smoked. Instead, he went to the gym four days a week.

So now what? You're a grown man...

"Alejandro? You okay out here?" Charlie stood, half in and half out of the shop, blocking the glass doorway. Dude looked like comic book Thor and Alejandro felt the usual pang of half-interested lust at the sight of the man whom he was slowly starting to call a friend. Not that he would poach Raquel's sweetheart. She'd rip off his heart and eat it for lunch. And besides, he didn't think Charlie swung that way. Alejandro swung pretty much every way, though his sex drive wasn't what it used to be, much to Shekinah's dismay.

"Alejandro?" The worry in Charlie's voice increased, and he stepped all the way out onto the sidewalk, hands in pockets, Ms. Marvel T-shirt straining over his very impressive pecs. Alejandro only recognized the young Ms. Marvel in her lightning bolt tunic and flowing red scarf because the alter ego of Pakistani teen Kamala Khan was one of his niece's favorites.

"Sorry. Woolgathering. How are you?"

Charlie stepped up beside Alejandro. He was of a similar

height, but much broader. "I'm fine. Shop's doing great. But I was trying to ask about you."

"I'm...fine." Alejandro exhaled again. "That's part of the problem. I can't figure out anything that's actually wrong. I mean, other than the usual state of the world stuff."

"And?"

"And... taking a break from consulting feels too easy. And as if that's not it. I don't know what I need to be paying attention to, and whether it's coming, or it's already here."

Charlie crossed his arms over his chest. "I hate it when you witches talk like that."

That shocked a laugh out of Alejandro. "Why's that?"

Charlie looked at him, assessing him with steady eyes. "Because when you say things like 'something's coming' it usually is. And that means my life's about to get harder again."

"You're right about that, hermano."

Charlie clapped him on the back. "Let's go inside. Your nephews are building quite a stack on the counter. You may need to do triage."

Charlie pulled the glass door open again, a phaser sounded, and Alejandro followed him on through.

Whatever may or may not be coming? It would have to wait. His sobrinos were the priority of the evening.

FREE BOOK

*Visit thorncoyle.com for a free short story collection and to
sign up for a monthly newsletter.*

*If you enjoyed this book, please consider telling a friend, or
leaving a short review at your favorite booksellers or on
GoodReads.*

Look for the next book in series: By Dark

ACKNOWLEDGMENTS

I give thanks to the cafés of my new hometown, Portland, Oregon. All you baristas are fine human beings.

Thanks also to Leslie Claire Walker, my intrepid first reader, to Dayle Dermatis, editor extraordinaire, to Lou Harper for my covers, and to my writing buddies for getting me out of the house.

Speaking of house...thanks as always to Robert and Jonathan.

Big, grateful shout out to the members of the Sorcery Collective for spreading the word!

And last...

Thanks to all the activists and witches working your magic in the world. This series is for you.

ABOUT THE AUTHOR

T. Thorn Coyle has been arrested at least four times. Buy them a cup of tea or a good whisky and they'll tell you about it.

Author of the *The Witches of Portland*, the alt-history urban fantasy series *The Panther Chronicles*, the novel *Like Water*, and two story collections, her multiple non-fiction books include *Sigil Magic for Writers, Artists & Other Creatives*, and *Evolutionary Witchcraft*.

Thorn's work appears in many anthologies, magazines, and collections. They have taught magical practice in nine countries, on four continents, and in twenty-five states.

An interloper to the Pacific Northwest U.S., Thorn stalks city streets, writes in cafes, loves live music, and talks to crows, squirrels, and trees.

Connect with Thorn:
www.thorncoyle.com